Commando-Colonel Islaen Connor and Admiral Sogan secured themselves in safety nets on the bridge of the starship *Fairest Maid*. The *Maid* fled an oncoming magnetic space storm. Such storms could easily destroy the mightiest transgalactic ships.

Islaen asked, "Can we outrun it?"

Sogan said, "We can try!"

But there was no escaping the cosmic tempest. Increasingly powerful currents swirled in mad disorder around the ship. Then the storm engulfed them and the universe exploded with incandescent blue light . . .

Ace Science Fiction books by P. M. Griffin

STAR COMMANDOS
STAR COMMANDOS: COLONY IN PERIL

P.M.GRIFFIN

ACE SCIENCE FICTION BOOKS
NEW YORK

This book is an Ace Science Fiction original edition,
and has never been previously published.

STAR COMMANDOS:
COLONY IN PERIL

An Ace Science Fiction Book / published by arrangement with
the author

PRINTING HISTORY
Ace Science Fiction edition / June 1987

Cover art by Miro.

For information address: The Berkley Publishing Group,
200 Madison Avenue, New York, New York 10016.

ISBN: 0-441-78043-1

Ace Science Fiction Books are published by
The Berkley Publishing Group,
200 Madison Avenue, New York, New York 10016.
PRINTED IN THE UNITED STATES OF AMERICA

To my mother, Mary Christine Griffin,
the first Terran to discover gurries.

ONE

THE SUPPLY DEPOT'S lack of luxury and polished decor did not trouble Varn Tarl Sogan. He expected none in a rim-world installation like this, and he preferred efficiency and a large stock from which to fill the *Maid*'s needs to any foredoomed attempt to copy the ways of the ancient, wealthy inner-system planets.

The shop was small and drab. Its walls were almost completely covered with boards listing the materials available, along with their prices and stock codes. Only one notice stating that other, less common items were also on hand broke the tedious columns. It drew the eye and invited inquiries.

The depot was fairly crowded. This part of the rim had become active in recent years. The local spacers were busy and had both the impetus and the credits to keep their ships well outfitted, and Horus, of Isis, along with her sister-world Set, was the governmental and service hub of the Sector. Most of her facilities were well utilized.

The patrons were a motley lot, the seed of many planets, and all had the look of tough competence that was the mark of those who flew the starlanes of any frontier Sector. Most of them knew one another, and they mingled freely while waiting to place or receive their orders, talking lightly or discussing more significant matters in lower tones. Word of a profitable charter could be picked up in such surroundings.

None of them approached the captain of the *Fairest Maid*. He was a stranger, and there was that about him, an aloofness, a custom of command, which kept most others at bay. It was a barrier for which he had reason to be immensely grateful since he had first become a wanderer of the starlanes, and for which he remained grateful although the greatest of his terrors was now laid to rest. There was still too much danger in the Federation for one of his race.

Sogan had little interest in his companions beyond that there were so many of them ahead of him, and he leaned back against the counter with an inward surge of irritation. Not very long ago, the population of an ultrasystem would have leaped to accomplish his will.

He quelled his annoyance. Those times were dead, and these last years had schooled him to patience, however little he might enjoy waiting. At least, fortune had so favored him that it was no longer necessary to demean himself by bartering as these others had to do. His official status now placed him on equal footing with other Navy officers and with the Stellar Patrol when it came to equipping himself and his ship.

This was a position in which he had never imagined to find himself—Varn Tarl Sogan sworn to the service of those his people had fought bitterly for so many years. The depot and its occupants faded as his mind buried itself once more in the strange, terrible series of events that had brought him to this place.

Not all that many years ago he had reigned as a war prince, in fact as well as in name, with star systems answering to his orders. His scarlet uniform had carried the insignia of Admiral, and he had commanded one of the Arcturian Empire's proudest and most successful combat fleets. In the final decade of the War, he had invaded Thorne of Brandine and had ruled her as head of his ultrasystem's occupation force for six years until the Arcturian surrender had forced withdrawal and sealed his own doom.

Pain and grief tore at him, but he did not attempt to banish the memories giving rise to them.

The shame of their cause's defeat had broken his commander's mind. Sogan had not recognized that, but when he had received the man's order to burn off Thorne, thereby annihilating all the life she sustained or might ever sustain in time to come, he had refused to do it.

Thorne had lived, and he had paid the full price for sparing her life. His people had needed a scapegoat on whom to vent their anger and pain in the aftermath of the first major defeat their race had ever suffered in all their long and warlike history—a defeat which, by their code, negated all the sacrifice and suffering and loss endured in their cause.

He had provided that. Disobedience to a battle order merited the death sentence for an enlisted man. For an officer, the penalty was infinitely harsher, and the full weight of the Empire's inflexible law had been thrown against him. Conviction and sentencing had come quickly and the implementation of that sentence more quickly still. He had been stripped of rank and of all else of worth in his life; his body had been broken under the whips of the fleet executioners and his supposed corpse cast adrift in space. The women of his harem had embraced their daggers in response to his disgrace and to the deaths of the children they had borne him, who had been slaughtered to eradicate the pollution of his seed from the race.

His head bowed slightly so that no shadow of his pain might be read by any of these strangers. Only a few months later, his commander's madness had been recognized. Had his trial been postponed even so long, his fate might have been otherwise. Even a few weeks' delay might have seen enough softening of his people's temper to have at least spared his children . . .

"You! What do you think you're doing here?" The challenge snapped Varn out of his reverie. He gave no sign that it had startled him as his head turned slowly to face its source, a well-muscled man whose square build and broad, full features proclaimed him to be an Albionan.

Sogan's cold eyes fixed him. "Nothing of concern to anyone save the personnel of this depot."

"Don't try any of your stiff-necked Arcturian tricks on me!"

A knot tightened in Varn's stomach, but his expression did not alter.

"Men have died for less." He had spoken quietly, but most of the others in the room, who had begun moving toward him at the voicing of the accusation, drew away once more. That was blaster talk, and this one did not strike any of them as a man who brooked much in the way of challenge or interference.

His accuser did not give ground. The Emperor's troops had never lacked nerve, and he had not expected this man to crumble before him. He had no intention of making this a duel. That would not be necessary. Once the other spacers were convinced of his race, they would come for him. The feelings roused in the recent War were still too fresh, too deep, to permit one of the Federation's old enemies to escape retribution.

"I saw enough instruction tapes during seven years with the Navy to know what Arcturians look like."

"Really?" a third voice interrupted contemptuously. "Commandos studied the originals, especially during years of penetration duty."

The spacer stared with almost ludicrous amazement at the slender young woman who had slipped unnoticed into the room.

"Commandos? You?"

Sogan's wry laughter rang in her mind despite the gravity of the situation. He, too, had been surprised to discover that so small a person was one of the elite, incredibly tough guerrillas.

Touching her thoughts to his in that form of communication they alone shared, she gave him a brief flash of reassurance before resuming her assault on his challenger.

"Commando-Colonel Islaen Connor. The man you're accusing happens to be my comrade. He's also a Navy Captain."

"But he's an . . ."

"Nearly every person born on Horus, as well as on a great many other planets, have olive complexions and dark hair. Quite a few of them won heroism citations for their work against the Empire, and nearly countless more died doing that work. I doubt any of them—or their kin—would take kindly to such labeling based on the way they happen to look."

She allowed the anger gripping her some rein. "If I were a Patrol agent, I'd slap charges of reckless endangerment on you, and I've half a mind to do it under my military authority. You could have roused enough feeling against this Federation citizen to have gotten him killed."

Easy, Colonel, Varn's mind warned her as he felt her fury

build. *I have met such challenges before without betraying myself.*

All the more to the Federation's shame! her thought retorted.

The former Admiral made her no answer although a chill began to rise within him. If only she had not come now! The crowd was still paying far too close attention to this scene. If she failed to turn their mood and the spacers attacked them as a mob, she would be trapped here with him. He might value his life more than he had a few months previously, but he infinitely preferred risking it alone to seeing Islaen Connor come into danger because of him.

If she was aware of the thoughts burning behind the shields he had raised around his mind to conceal them, she gave no sign of it. Islaen broadened the focus of her attention to include the others present in the room.

"Now listen to me, all of you. I've probably had closer and longer contact with Arcturians than any of you. I raided them, and I lived and fought for four years on a planet invaded and controlled by them, but now the War's over. Maybe citizens of the Empire can't enter Federation space in number, but individuals may, should any desire to do so. Only a handful of specified men have been exempted from that privilege."

"A handful of monsters!" someone spat from the rear of the room.

The Commando's eyes speared him. "A very few out of all their millions. They're worthy of hate, aye—most of you can't even appreciate how much—but remember our own planets' histories before you blame all their kind."

Once more, she addressed the entire crowd. "You might as well not be looking for Arcturians at every planetfall. They don't like to be reminded of their defeat, nor are they likely to put themselves in danger of humiliation or worse by venturing into our territory. Bear that in mind before any of you accost someone again because he has some fancied, or actual, physical resemblance to our recent enemies."

Islaen said no more. She had kept open her receptors, the senses of her mind through which she received emotions emanating from those around her, throughout the incident and knew that the danger was over. Her harangue had worked, that and the mystique of her unit and the awe generated by the place she had gained within it. It was a well-known fact that Commandos earned their rank, and it was equally well known that only the very best of them had been asked to remain in the greatly reduced peacetime force. Every one of the spacers ranged before her realized that her record had to be nothing short of spectacular.

Embryonic mob anger had given way to a sheepish embarrassment, strongest of all in the man who had begun the trouble. The Albionan seemed to shrink in on himself, but then he sighed and came closer to Sogan.

"Look, Captain, you have every right to deck me and a lot more . . ."

Because the situation demanded it and more so because he appreciated that these spacers did not make less of themselves easily, Varn allowed a smile to soften his features.

"Nothing came of it, thanks to Colonel Connor. It is not the first time such a misunderstanding has happened. The likeness is there, and it has even served to my advantage on occasion."

"All the same, I am sorry. I'm Solman Abbott of Albion, master of the *Mary Jane*."

"Sogan of the *Fairest Maid*."

A dead silence filled the room, and he caught the hiss of more than one sharply drawn breath. The work of settling the Amonites in on Jade of Kuan Yin had been in full swing for the last several months, and nearly every starship in the Sector would have had some share in it. As a result, the details of the colonists' story would be fairly fresh in the crews' minds.

"The man who fought those bugs on the ground, and then had to walk through the whole hoard of them?" Solman gasped.

"Colonel Connor drew me away from them before I had traveled far."

"And I might have been responsible—"

"Forget it. I played upon my appearance there, if you recall that part of the tale."

Several of the spacers grinned. By claiming to be an Arcturian, he had forced the developers of the illegal colony to sign both a full confession and a compensation agreement for the people they had so greatly wronged.

The Albionan glanced at the woman. "I'm sorry, Colonel. I should have known your name as well."

She only laughed. "My role wasn't nearly as dramatic. Now, how about getting back to business? I really am eager to get the *Maid* outfitted and off-world."

"You're going to Jade?" one of the others asked and then reddened; one did not question Commandos about their work.

The Colonel smiled. "Aye, as a matter of fact, but for our own pleasure. We find ourselves with a little free time and one of my former comrades is there serving as liaison between the Amonites and the Settlement Board. We're anxious to see him."

TWO

THEY WERE NOT delayed long. The others drew back, letting them go ahead, and they soon had the few items they needed.

Take them, Islaen Connor's mind instructed.

The war prince smoothly swept the packages into his arms as if that had been his original intention. *More trouble?*

That question was almost unnecessary. The Commando had joined him here specifically so that she could carry the microswitches. She would not lightly risk having them damaged by putting them in with the rest of the packages.

Maybe. We defused that mob itself, but not everyone comprising it was convinced. A few of those spacers radiated considerable hostility at first, if you recall, then most of it vanished abruptly.

Sogan nodded. Although he could not himself receive readings from other members of his species, Islaen had kept her receptors linked with his so that he had also been aware of the emotions of those around them. He remembered that dark feeling now. It had been cut off suddenly and not softened or altered, which indicated that those emitting it had left the depot. He had vaguely realized that their hostility could still mean trouble, but the more immediate situation around them had held his attention, and he had forgotten the unpleasant touches. Fortunately, the woman had not.

His failure angered and embarrassed him, but Varn realized the lapse was natural enough. Not very many months ago, he had not even realized such reading was possible, not until his talent had awakened under the pressures put on him on Visnu. He was not yet so completely accustomed to his own power to pick up the transmissions of animals or to decipher the information he received from Islaen to always be able to respond instinctively or accurately, as he would to warnings delivered by his more mundane senses.

With the Colonel, it was different. Her gift had surfaced early, during the first weeks following her enlistment. She had been smart enough to keep quiet about it, and it had served her and her cause well throughout the long years of the War and in her battles since the great conflict had ended. She was as used to relying upon it as she was to depending on her eyes and ears and was not likely to ignore any warning it carried to her.

The man followed her outside, carefully settling his burdens so that his right hand remained free. *Did you get everything?* his thought asked as he came up beside her.

Aye. I put it all in the flier before heading for the depot. Her eyes darkened. *I wish we didn't have to go so far.*

More than the distance was bothering her. Islaen Connor had a guerrilla's dislike for the wide, coverless vehicle facility and an even stronger distrust of its single, shadowed pedestrian entryway.

Sogan read her concern easily enough. *You fear an ambush?*

It's a possibility, she responded grimly. *They won't try anything on the main streets, but that blasted underpass would be ideal for making trouble.*

I know. Something in the way he said that made her look sharply at the former Admiral.

He caught her unvoiced question and gave a mental shrug. *Thorne's Resistance taught me to fear such places.* He remained silent for a few moments. *Maybe it would be wise to go directly to the* Maid *and let the military pick up the flier for us.*

No way! Islaen caught herself, then smiled. She had stepped right into that.

Sogan chuckled. *It was only a suggestion, Colonel. I somehow did not imagine it would appeal to you.*

Appeal or not, the woman thought, she had best consider it. She had never claimed to be immune to interservice rivalry, but now was not the time to let it rule her judgment. After several moments' reflection, she decided to continue on, at least until circumstances showed that to be impractical.

Maybe we'll wind up acting on it, friend, she told him at the end of that time, *but bad feeling doesn't necessarily mean an assault. Let's be certain we need help from the Regulars before calling for it.* She grimaced. *Otherwise the story'll be all over Horus that Commandos start at their own footfalls. Besides,* she added practically, *I bought a few perishables and want to get them stowed as soon as possible.*

He laughed. *Good enough, Colonel Connor.* The lightness left him. *We are nearing the vehicle facility. Can you pick anything up?*

Just ahead of them, the steady line of buildings was broken, and the sidewalk on which they were traveling veered sharply to the left. It began to descend as well, flowing downward on a smooth, steep grade until it seemed to disappear into a dark tunnel about a hundred feet from the turnoff.

The woman sent her mind forward, probing the blackness beyond for any sign of potential foes. *Several people are in there. They seem to be waiting, and their mood's not good, but that's about all I can get. Let's go a bit closer.*

Islaen gave a warning hiss as they turned off the main street. *It's them! Three of them, I think.*

Waiting for us?

I can't read minds, just emotions, but who else?—I don't like what they're radiating at all.

He nodded slowly. She had linked with him again, and the hatred in these transmissions was dangerously strong. Men such as these spacers could kill readily when driven far less severely. *What do we do, Colonel?*

The Commando gazed thoughtfully into the gloom just beyond them. *I don't think they plan outright murder. At worst, we risk having the circuits smashed out of us. . . .*

Out of me. I am the one they want.

Not if I don't keep out of it—which I won't, she told him dryly.

She gazed thoughtfully at the underpass entrance. *If we can take them, it'll be to our good. We base out of Horus, and we're going to have to continue using her facilities. That may not prove easy if these thugs drive us off now.*

Aye, Sogan agreed somberly. *Word of it would spread, and with it their suspicion and hatred of me—I say chance it.*

Even as his mind gave her his decision, he carefully set his packages down beside the path. *No use risking these. If everything goes well, we can retrieve them later. If it does not, we will not need any additional burdens.*

Despite the deep blackness of its entrance as seen from the bright world outside, the underpass was not actually dark. Isis' rays poured through the open ends in sufficient strength that no daytime lighting was deemed necessary by those in charge of the facility beyond. The center of the long passage was dim and gray, but the three shadowy figures lounging casually against the wall were clearly visible.

They looked to be space hounds by their dress. The Colonel did not recognize any of them, but the touch of their minds identified them. They had been in the depot when Solman Abbott had challenged Sogan and had left it in hot anger.

They were not outright pirates or anything of that ilk, she judged after several moments' closer study. The vicious, casual violence marking the minds of all that kind was not present here.

That was not necessary for them to represent a decided threat to the two Navy officers. Spacers working the ever-expanding rim of the ultrasystem were a tough, hard lot, well accustomed to managing their own affairs and fighting their own battles. They had to be to function at all in the unpatrolled, often pirate-infested starlanes linking the outermost colonies. Their life was hard, and it bred into them a raw, direct brand of justice and the tendency to quick, sharp response to any real or fancied wrong against them. Once aroused, as they now were, they were not likely to turn from the action they had determined to take.

The spacers spotted the newcomers in the same moment that they themselves had been seen. They straightened and stepped out onto the narrow footpath so that they stood like a barrier across it.

There could be no doubting their purpose, and Islaen knew she had little hope of talking them down, not with the level of raw fury they were radiating. They meant to have their vengeance on Sogan. All the same, she was resolved to avoid an actual fight if she could. There was no point to risking death or serious injury unnecessarily.

She waited until she was within easy speaking distance before signaling her companion to halt and stopping herself. Her eyes were cold and hard as they met those of each of the three in turn.

"I'd suggest letting us pass. There are some pretty stiff penalties for assaulting military personnel."

"I don't see any uniforms, Commando or Regular," the apparent leader retorted. He was playing for time, she saw, trying to distract them and hold their attention until his companions could get the jump on them.

"Commandos and those who work with us rarely wear them," the woman replied evenly, as if unaware of his intention. "We wouldn't live very long in our line of business if we did."

"You have all the right answers, don't you? Except your partner there isn't so easy to explain away."

"No one has to explain his role in the Federation." This time her voice was cold, deadly to one capable of reading the undertones rippling in it.

Her opponent's eyes flickered to the former Admiral.

"Put it on freeze, Beautiful! We lost a lot of friends to his kind, and we plan to settle part of that score. Now. Stay out of it or you'll get the same yourself. And maybe a bit more besides," he added significantly as he ran his eyes along the lines of her lithe body.

Even as he spat that out, the spacer launched himself at the Arcturian. But Islaen's counterattack came even faster. The edge of her hand caught the man sharply and squarely in the throat and he went down, gagging at her feet.

The others started to move as well, but a glaring stream of angry energy crackled across the space separating them, and they froze in place. They stood staring at Sogan's blaster as if they could not believe a weapon could come into a man's hand in so minute a span of time.

For a moment he said nothing but only watched them, all the while holding the blaster well out before him, his fingers dangerously tight on its trigger.

"Guerrillas are more readily recognized by their battle skill than by their garments," he said at last, then glanced at the felled man. "Will that one live?" he asked the Commando-Colonel.

"Aye. His windpipe isn't crushed. I controlled the blow."

His voice became cold as he fixed his attention once more on the others. "If I were what you took me to be, I should burn you as you stand for this. Unfortunately, a Navy officer lacks that freedom of action, so clear—fast—and take that refuse on the ground with you, or I shall forget the control demanded of me and crisp you for a fact."

None of the would-be attackers had any fight left. They picked up their still-choking comrade and fled the underpass, only too glad to escape with their lives.

THREE

SOGAN WAITED UNTIL he was certain the spacers would not return and then went back outside to reclaim his supplies. He rejoined the woman a few minutes later.

They will not be back.

No.—You handled that beautifully.

It was obvious what had to be done.

There was a tightness on him, and she sighed to herself. It had been an ugly incident, one which had to be even more distasteful to this man than it had been to her. Space scum like that were vermin in his eyes. Any interaction with them, much less a near brawl, would be degrading to one of his station, and Varn Tarl Sogan had not set aside so much of his past that he did not feel soiled by the exchange.

They wasted no time in passing through the remainder of the passage. It opened into the huge parking field servicing this part of Horus' capital. Vehicles seemed to stretch out before them like the stars forming the arms of the galaxy, but they had been lucky enough to secure a space near the entrance, and they soon located their own craft.

Both remained silent while they stowed their purchases in the Commando's deceptively common-looking flier, but Islaen's mind sought the former Admiral's again once they had taken their own places.

That must have been painful for you.

Frightening, he answered frankly. *I am an Arcturian, after all, and a war prince at that.*

With every right—

I know, but there are too many who would dispute it, whether I carry Thorne's citizenship and the Federation's or not.

Her head lowered for a moment. *Most people have never seen an Arcturian save in a newstape now and then. There weren't even many prisoners until right at the very end. To the vastly greater part of us, civilians and soldiers alike, we fought ships and weapons, defeated them or died through them, not the men flying and wielding them. I suppose that's one reason why the hatred's so strong. You weren't really perceived as human at all, merely as a vast, invading force trying to drive the life and light and freedom away from us. Most of the few personal reports we got came secretly from overrun planets, and they were frequently grim in the extreme.* She looked at him somberly for a moment. *Usually, they were all too accurate.*

I know. Occupation duty was rarely a welcome assignment. Officers resented it even without having to cope with Resistance activity. Still, your people do wrong us. Most Arcturians tried to fight cleanly by our lights, even as your soldiers did.

The woman realized suddenly that she had heard Arcturians discuss Federation tactics and the merits of certain officers where rank or deeds had been sufficient to draw the attention of the Empire's intelligence to individuals, but she had never actually heard them speak of their opponents themselves.

Did your side have a more accurate image of us? Islaen asked after a moment. She felt some hesitation in raising that question, fearing to tear open old wounds. Varn too carefully avoided any mention of his former career and comrades, not to be pained by the memory of them. Still, she did want to know if the Federation was alone in this particular injustice.

Sogan was silent for some time before responding. *No. No, it was no more accurate and no less emotional.* He paused. *There was contempt at first, I understand, but that had disappeared long before I enlisted for active duty. By then, there was no doubting the skill or courage of those we faced.*

Sogan frowned. It was difficult to explain this attitude of his people, to make it comprehensible to her. Like most such feelings, it had not been formed by any conscious effort, and he was not even certain how much of his theory was an actual explanation for it.

Few of us had any personal contact with your soldiers, and fewer wanted any. The Federation is a mongrel system to our eyes, comprised of the populations of numerous planets, many with no Terran roots whatsoever. Some are not human at all or are so far mutated from prototype as to be scarcely recognizable as such. All were represented in your Navy, a Navy staffed, not by carefully bred professionals, but by individuals from every conceivable lifeway, every caste. The very basis of your existence, the principles guiding you, were both totally alien and utterly unacceptable to us.

We found it difficult to believe at first that the Federation could fight at all, much less bring our advance to a standstill and then start to drive us back, as you eventually did. As it gradually became apparent that defeat at your hands was at least conceivable, the natural loathing we felt for such an unnatural and uncontrolled system intensified into a fierce hatred.

His hands spread in a gesture of helplessness, which he tried to cover by taking hold of the flier's control rod.

In that response, my race has shown itself not very different from the Federation's many. —As with your people, it burned in some with great virulence, usually in those who kept farthest from the battle line, he added with a rare display of bitterness.

You were never one of those, Islaen said softly.

I was fortunate in that I had always faced highly competent opponents both in space and later on Thorne. Particularly the Thornens. They were a fine, attractive people in themselves, and they fought such a war against us as I would wish Arcturians to wage were our positions reversed. Had I been faced with vermin like those three we just set running, the old prejudices would probably have been powerfully reinforced. No Arcturian would feel anything but contempt for them.

He fell silent for a long while, and she could sense that his closed thoughts, those in the deep inner part of his mind beyond her power to probe and read, were troubled.

The man glanced at her at last. *There is another side to us, Islaen, one that does not revolve around the eternal waging of war. . . .* He sighed then and fixed his attention on the vehicle-packed road before them.

His mind was shut, sealed against her, and the woman felt

her heart grow heavy. It had been like this so often of late, ever since they had left the planet Noreen.

When they reached the *Maid*, Islaen Connor boarded at once, leaving Sogan to install the new valves and the microswitches they had bought. The remainder of their purchases consisted of foodstuffs, and these she proceeded to store.

She worked quickly, without giving much of her mind to the task. Her thoughts were on her own affairs, and they were bleak.

She had been a fool to ever take Varn Tarl Sogan for her consort. . . . The woman smiled a little despite her inner pain. That was his word, but a considerable degree of formality seemed proper, more than proper, natural, when dealing with the war prince even if only in thought.

A bitter knife twisted in her heart, and she battled to chain it before she inadvertently broadcast her trouble to Sogan.

This was entirely her own fault. Islaen knew she should have realized that there must be difficulties in a relationship with such a man as this, a man with Varn's background and his history of loss. She had realized it, but there had been no problems, no shadow between them, until after they had lifted from that belated and apparently accursed visit to her homeworld.

The former Admiral had been wonderful there. He had exhibited not only the unwavering courtesy she would always expect from him but a charm of manner that had soon completely won everyone over to him. That had been no minor accomplishment, either. Most of her relatives and their neighbors regretted and, in some cases, resented that she had accepted this stranger for her husband instead of Jake Karmikel, himself a Noreenan and her comrade through all her years in the service.

Sogan, in turn, had seemed to like her people. Maybe he truly did, but even so, his caste training might well be rising up to overpower that liking and with it his love and his respect for her.

Her family, like the bulk of Noreen's citizens, were agrarians, menials to Arcturian thought, beings with no worth beyond the services they could provide for the warrior caste. He had known the lifeway from which she had come but had always regarded her as a warrior and an officer. Had the actual meeting with her people and observation of them altered that perception, so that he now believed his marriage with her demeaning?

Her eyes closed, but her body remained projectile straight. She had to know for certain. If it were true, she would have to find a way to release him.

A sob rose within her, but the woman quelled it. Strength was required from her now. The whole burden lay on her, for Varn Tarl Sogan would never of himself violate the vows he had given to her, and she loved him too much, cared for him too much, to hold him bound in a partnership he detested.

"Islaen!"

The Commando turned quickly, startled to hear Varn's voice. They rarely used speech when they were alone, not since discovering that they could communicate directly through thought.

The Arcturian saw her pallor and the shade of misery she had not been quick enough to chase from her expression. "Why do you close your mind to me, hide your pain from me?"

Wordlessly, she lowered the shields she had kept about herself, ashamed and fearful as to what his response would be. It had been hers to trust him.

She felt his anger and hurt, but both were almost instantly swallowed by sheer incredulity.

You could believe that? You could even imagine it? he asked in the manner now customary with them. *Islaen, you are my very soul and the savior of my soul, having given me life in the place of the existence in which I was wallowing. Whatever allowed such madness entry into your mind?*

You've been so guarded since our visit to Noreen. I thought, feared . . .

Islaen shuddered and slipped into his arms. *I wronged you. I'm sorry.*

Sogan held her for a few moments, letting his love pour into her. *Your people are not you,* he said at the end of that time, *but they do have my respect. Many of them fought and fought well. That would not have been the case with Arcturian menials.* He grimaced. *They would not have been given the chance to do so.*

Varn looked at her gravely. *Meeting with your people, the kin and associates whom you have so often described and whom you love, was not distasteful to me, but Arcturians, too, can laugh and make new kindred welcome. I wish that I might have brought you there.*

All the loss and longing welled up in him, and he quickly severed the contact between them lest she be pained by it.

"I did not want you to realize I harbored such feelings."

"How could you not," she whispered, "being the man you are?" Islaen clung to him. His arms closed more tightly around her.

"Islaen . . ."

"I was so sure I was losing you," she whispered. "That I'd already lost you."

"I am no child to withdraw from such a commitment as we have made."

This was not the answer to give her! Sogan cursed himself for his insensitivity to her need and her unhappiness. By all the Federation's gods, what was the matter with him? Their very thoughts, their minds, were linked. How could he have failed her like this?

"I love you," he told her fiercely as his fear of losing her waxed high within him. "Nothing can alter that."

The Arcturian stroked her rich auburn hair, trying to calm the violence of the emotion, the regret and guilt, rending his heart and mind.

This should teach us caution, Islaen Connor, he said thoughtfully at last. *We are too accustomed, both of us, to the demands of command, the need to hold our own council, to hide our uncertainties. There must be no more of that between us.*

No, the woman agreed softly, although she privately doubted either of them would be able to hold to that resolve, not fully.

She freed herself with a laugh that was only partly forced. *Come, Admiral! I wasn't making it up when I said I was anxious to see Jake, and we can't appropriate an infinite amount of time for visiting old friends.*

The Arcturian frowned. *You were very free in giving our destination, for a Commando.*

Aye, she responded, her eyes sparkling. *It doesn't do the Amonites any harm to have it known that they're not forgotten merely because they're on their own world at last.*

FOUR

ISLAEN POURED A second cup of jakek and returned to the minute mess cabin to enjoy it in peace. Varn might choke down his breakfast and race off to his precious drive engines, but for her part, she liked to take her meals slowly and in comfort. She had known little enough opportunity for that since her enlistment and was not about to waste any chance given to her.

Suddenly, the cup flew out of her hand as a violent jerk flung her lengthwise along the bench. A second jolt nearly rolled her under the table. The Colonel braced herself before a third could hit, but none came.

Varn, what's wrong? her mind demanded.

Nothing!

Despite that curt assurance, she hastened to the drive room. Nothing seemed terribly amiss, although one of the casings was open, revealing an incredibly complex series of wires and microchips. Sogan was bent over this, swearing softly with great fluency in his own language.

Islaen smiled to herself. He must be very deeply engrossed and very annoyed to forget that she spoke Arcturian quite as well and as thoroughly as he.

She remained silent, not interrupting him until she saw his expression lighten. *You've got it figured out?*

He looked up. *Aye, or I believe so. I think I tightened a couple of the valves too much, and they could not act freely enough when I tried to let her out. These hookups your Navy people put in are ingenious, but they require a light hand in managing them.*

I'll leave you at it, then, but please no more acrobatics if you can help it.

I hope not, he agreed, rubbing a bruised elbow. *Our new maneuverability is intended to down our enemies, not ourselves.*

It was nearly three hours later when Islaen interrupted Sogan once more. *Varn, are you nearly through?*

Aye.

Good. Finish up as soon as you can. We're getting some readings that I don't particularly like.

He frowned. There was a tenseness in that more indicative of concern than her actual words. *Which indicators?*

The magnetics. It may be nothing, but I think you should have a look.

Let me see them now. Instinctively, the man put his hand against the wall to steady himself as Islaen linked her eyes with his.

His balance adjusted after a moment, and he scanned the gauges on which the woman's attention was focused. *Not noteworthy readings in themselves,* he remarked. *When did the activity start?*

Twenty minutes ago. It's been rising steadily since.

Keep watching them. I'll be up as soon as I seal everything down here.

Praise the Spirit of Space that he had finished, the former Admiral thought as he slipped the drive casings back into place and reset their seals. He would not normally have felt much concern over such low-level magnetics, but this section of space had a very bad reputation for suddenly born, fast-rising storms, sometimes of considerable violence, and it would not have been well to be caught in any such disturbance with a partially operational ship.

It would not be well to be caught in one at all. Even relatively minor magnetic turbulence could shake a small vessel like the *Fairest Maid* to the full of her endurance. The worst of them, the mighty upheavals of space, second only to a supernova letting go at close proximity, could be death to the largest transgalactics.

Even in the few minutes it took him to reach the bridge, the readings had worsened, very slightly but still perceptibly.

Sogan looked at them grimly as he strapped himself into the pilot's seat. *You set the antimagnetics?*

Aye, before I called for you.

Good.

The Commando quietly slipped into her own safety nets. *We're in for a blow?*

Maybe. We would do well to prepare for one. He glanced at the gauges once more. *At least, we have no debris field to worry about.*

She nodded. Such a storm could turn space rubble into missiles of awesome speed and force. *Delectize as well?*

It might be a good idea. This region has a record of discharges.

He opened his transceiver on general beam and broadcast a warning of the potential disturbance, giving their coordinates and a preliminary assessment of the situation.

That should keep other ships out of trouble, he told his companion as he closed the transmission.

Neither had any doubt by then that a magnetic storm was indeed building around them. The signs had become all too clear to be misread, and the fact that it was rising so rapidly boded very ill for them when it broke for a fact.

Can we outrun it, get to its perimeter at least? Islaen asked.

We are about to try, Colonel.

For two hours, the *Fairest Maid* fled before the growing turbulence, but in the end they realized they would not be able to escape it, not entirely.

Varn was forced to give an ever greater portion of his attention to avoiding the increasingly powerful currents swirling around them in mad disorder, currents that could catch up his ship and toss her through space as if she were no more than a pebble. If once he lost control even for the barest moment, or if the *Maid*'s antimagnetics should be breached . . .

He drove her sharply to three o'clock. A crosscurrent struck her squarely, almost tore her from him, but he jerked her back nearly upon herself, out of the eddy forming in the place they had occupied an instant before.

His lips compressed until they and the skin around them were paper white. She could not have done that a few months before. The Navy's equipment was proving out thus far, but what if any of it failed, or if he were not good enough to manage the *Maid*'s new capabilities, if he did not react as he must during this emergency? Every moment brought a demand for decision, and one single error would be their death.

The Arcturian pressed the controls again, then his breath caught as all the universe around them lit up suddenly with incandescent blue light.

The discharge held for slightly better than three seconds and was of sufficient intensity to be perceptible to instruments in every bordering star system.

Both he and his companion sat frozen, not daring to move lest they touch some metal part of the ship. Even in here, the eerie crackling of the delectizers was clearly audible as they struggled to neutralize the almost incomprehensible wave of energy battering at them. They were strong, but some leakage, enough to turn the vessel into a temporary agent of death, was all too possible.

Total failure could also occur, but in that event, they would do well to seek the release the rampaging electricity offered. The starship would be dead in space, and even if she could by some cruel stroke of fortune avoid destruction in the turbulence trapping her, there would be almost no hope of restoring her fused systems. Death would be inevitable, and very slow.

The *Maid*'s defenses did hold, and when the normal blackness of the starlanes returned to the universe outside, Sogan's shoulders straightened. They were most unlikely to be so fortunate a second time.

He had always been known as a wily, cautious commander, careful of his ships and the men flying them, but he had also earned the name of a war leader who could in need move with a daring brilliance that had often brought disaster to Federation officers unfortunate enough to oppose him. It was that last which was required of him now, and he set his directionals to twelve o'clock, then pushed the speed control to the very maximum.

The *Fairest Maid* leaped forward, bucking as she skipped across a blessedly narrow stream running parallel to her new course.

Sogan did not turn her or permit her velocity to drop, although he knew such a maneuver could easily doom them within minutes. He was gambling that they were near enough to the perimeter of the storm that they would soon reach it. There, they would face an even greater challenge, but nothing to that inherent in remaining where they were. The fury of this tempest had barely begun to build. The *Maid* would never be able to stand against it at its height, nor, he believed, would she be able to hold long enough to work her way out slowly.

There's a shimmering ahead, Islaen observed. Her eyes were fixed on the viewer screen where the data gathered by the sensitive scanners were translated into visual images.

The man nodded. *The edge if we are in luck.*

It had better be, he thought grimly. The *Maid* was now vibrating in a way that would send a chill through the heart of any spacer. She was still ploughing valiantly onward, but the forces hammering and tearing at her were immense. She would not be able to keep on much longer.

The edge of the storm was before them!

Sogan slowed a little to give himself time to study it. The forces holding these vast interstellar cyclones together were almost incomprehensibly powerful, and it was no simple matter to pass out of one of them into unaffected space.

Direct frontal assault would be pointless, he decided. The *Fairest Maid*'s engines simply did not possess the strength to break through, yet to wait longer was even more perilous.

The *Maid* could not do it unaided, but if she rode with one of these mighty energy streams threatening her, used its strength to boost her own drive, she should just be able to pierce the shimmering barrier. Failure would be the end of them, of course, but that would have been the case had he erred in any of his judgments thus far. He dared not play the coward now and withdraw from decision, for to do nothing would assuredly be fatal.

Hang on, Colonel!

The starship's speed doubled, trebled, as he found and joined with the current he sought. On and on she flew until she struck hard against what seemed to be a solid substance. She struggled to penetrate it, her every seam creaking and screaming under the stress. Her tubes shook and heated in a manner that told all too graphically how close they were to complete blowout.

Suddenly, all pressure was gone from her, and the *Maid* shot through a wonderfully clear and calm space like some flare spat from the heart of an exploding star.

Sogan brought her down to a sane speed and then took readings from the navputer.

Not too bad, considering.

He called in their coordinates and gave a full report to Horus on the intensity of the storm and his impression as to its probable duration and course.

Sogan smiled a little tightly as he closed the transmission. The operator's amazement at their survival had been quite as open as the warmth of her congratulations. For a while there, he had not held much hope that they would come through it himself.

His hands slid slowly to his sides, and he slumped back in his chair. For a moment, his eyes remained closed, but then he opened them and fixed them on the universe beyond the narrow visual observation panels. Gradually, his expression relaxed as the star-bright infinity outside began to work its magic on him.

How magnificent it is, Islaen, he murmured at last. *Even at its most perilous, it is wondrous beyond our ken.*

He sighed. *I often wish the* Maid *could have a transparent skin so that I might truly feel part of it all again.*

Again?

Sogan nodded, smiling wistfully. *Aye. One of my residences, my favorite, was a satellite fashioned entirely of silicate crystal, save for a defensive core. I was born there and spent every moment I could within it. There had been time for that before the tide of the War turned so conclusively against us.*

He sighed again and turned back to his instruments. *I do not suppose such a place could even exist in Federation space. That surrounding my homeworld is uncommonly still, with no rubble to threaten delicate structures. Five generations of my family used that palace, and never once did we have to retire to the core.*

No shooting stars, she mused. *I should miss those.*

No magnetic storms, either, he countered. *Come, Colonel Connor. We have work in front of us yet before we planet on Jade of Kuan Yin.*

FIVE

THEY HAD LOST little actual time despite the delay the storm and resulting broad detour had caused them. It had provided an excellent testing of most of the equipment the Navy had installed in the *Maid* after their battle over Astarte, and the few remaining tests did not hold them long.

Sogan was feeling decidedly pleased with himself and with his ship by the time Kuan Yin began to assume prominence in their distance viewer.

Everything worked like a technician's dream, he gloated to his companion. *Now, only the weapons and defenses remain for trial.*

Don't sound so wistful. We're not likely to be left at peace for very long. I wouldn't be in any hurry calling trouble down on us.

Perish the thought, Colonel, but I cannot help wishing we had had some of this to greet those pirates.

It would've been handy, right enough, but we gave them an effective reception with what we did have. That's probably what moved the brass to give us so much, in fact. They figured we'd put it to excellent use.

I have no intention of hunting up any more pirate armadas to test their playthings, he told her dryly.

The woman's eyes sparkled. *After what happened on Visnu*

and then on Astarte, they probably believe difficulties come to us of their own accord.

There was little further conversation between the pair. Kuan Yin and her system were now close enough to stand as readily observable entities, and they were eager to study them.

The sun-star was big, and both thought her extremely well named. She was extraordinarily lovely, gold just barely tinted with green, and her fires were soft, exhibiting none of the violence characteristic of most of her sisters.

Four planets orbited her. All were large, and all were blessed with an abundance of small and moderately-sized satellites. The innermost one, Jade, was their destination.

The planet was not impressive at the first sighting. She looked blue, indicating a heavy water cover, and showed a good speckling of clouds, but she lacked the magic seen in so many other worlds.

Well, the Amonites would not mind that lack if she would work with them and allow them to work with her. Besides, it was a deceptive impression, the Commando knew. This was, in fact, a varied and attractive planet of seas and highlands, hill country, vast savannahs, tremendous river plains, deltas, and some swamps. Of the features normally stirring to the human spirit, only great belts of forest were missing.

Islaen had little opportunity to examine her more closely. Even now, Sogan was in contact with Jade's guidance tower, and soon they would be making their planeting approach.

Varn set the delicate-looking needle-nose down with barely a tremor to tell her occupants that they were on Jade's surface.

He had scarcely deactivated her engines before releasing his safety nets and coming to his feet. There was no need to adjust for either gravity or atmosphere here, both of which were Terra-normal, optimal for his species' comfort.

As quickly as the Arcturian moved, he had only just lifted the *Maid*'s seals when the transceiver clamored for his attention.

His companion's face brightened marvelously, and he knew she was picking up Jake Karmikel's familiar pattern.

"Aye, Jake?" he asked as soon as he reached the mike.

"How—Oh, bother the good Colonel's gift anyway!—Mind if I come on board?"

"Not at all. Welcome. We are on the bridge."

Islaen Connor did not confine herself to a verbal greeting when the tall redhead appeared in the cabin door a few minutes later. She sprang into his arms with a crow of delight.

"It's great to see you again! The Commandos haven't been the same since you were foolish enough to retire!"

Karmikel lifted her from the deck and spun her in a complete circle before setting her on her feet again. "They're still treating you all right by the look of it."

Sogan watched the exchange with amusement and also with a touch of envy. He couldn't bring himself to greet anyone so, to be so exuberant, not even with this woman whose life was bound with his and whose mind so often shared thought with his own.

Jake released the Colonel at last and turned to the other in a more subdued manner. The Arcturian took his hand although he still had to school himself to do so naturally. The Federation custom was unknown in his ultrasystem. No one amongst his own people would have dared touch him at all save the Emperor himself and his heir-son and, in the privacy of his own residence, the war prince's closest kin.

"Welcome to Jade," the redhead told them.

"Thanks," the woman responded. "You're looking grand, Jake. Thinking of adopting her?"

He shook his head. "Not me. I'm an irredeemable space hound. She is nice, though. Not our present camp particularly, but on the whole."

"What is she like?" Sogan asked. "We read a synopsis, but that merely mentioned a varied surface and abundant flora and fauna, all from the more common categories."

"Jade's a good world and will provide a good living to those willing to work hard and adapt themselves to her ways. The wildlife, plant and animal, do follow familiar patterns, and it's with some of the latter that the Amonites plan to establish themselves. There's little in the way of insect types to trouble them, much to everyone's relief."

Islaen gave him a look of mild surprise. "I thought they were crop farmers."

"So they were on Visnu because she offered them nothing in the way of a choice, but they declared a definite preference for stock work. Jade gives them the best opportunity for that while allowing them to maintain an extremely low ecological impact, and that was one of the major factors influencing their choice of her. Gaea will be here shortly and will be delighted to explain.

He laughed softly. "Brace yourselves for a long lecture. The Councilwoman is one with her constituents in their excitement over what they hope to build here."

The Commando looked swiftly upon him. She had detected worry on him while he had been speaking, but the taint had been fleeting and was now completely gone. Before she could press him, the transceiver sounded once more, and the head of the colonists' Directing Council requested permission to come aboard.

Gaea of Amon had lost nothing of her bearing or strength in the time since they had last seen her. She was a woman in her race's middle years, accustomed to public service, and had proven to be a fine leader during her people's attempts to settle Visnu of Brahmin and the near-disaster of the ravager assault. She had been a wise guiding force during the trial of the developers who had deceived them, and also in the choosing of their new planet. She was now ably continuing her role as the Amonites struggled to change their position from that of first-ship colonists to permanent, independent residents. The pride on her was that of earned worth and the sense of accomplishment, an open pride that did not lessen any other.

Her smile was glad when she gave greeting to the pair. "No one else in all the ultrasystem could be more welcome on Jade," she told them warmly.

She favored them with yet another smile. "I understand you two are to be congratulated. Yours is a union most well made. May you have joy in it."

They thanked her, and then all four left the bridge for the *Maid*'s small but comfortably appointed crew's cabin where they might talk in greater ease.

When they were settled, Islaen turned inquisitively to the Councilwoman. "Jake tells us you've decided to concentrate your primary efforts on working with some of the native animals."

Gaea nodded. "Aye, on one particular species. They have dictated our future lifestyle, as a matter of fact." She leaned a little forward. "The creatures in question are migratory, herd-dwelling grazers which exist in vast numbers. We have given them a name that translates into goldbeast in Basic. It was mating season when we first saw them, and the cows were a vivid, true yellow color."

"You'll try to tame some of them, or take calves young enough for training?"

The other shook her head. "Not as you mean. That was the course proposed for us, to settle in the river plain where the herd is now, take a number of the animals, and raise crops to feed ourselves and them in the fertile soil there, but we have decided to travel with the goldbeasts instead."

Sogan betrayed no sign of surprise, but Islaen's brows raised. "That's a somewhat drastic course, isn't it?"

"Not really, and it was the one followed by Amon's citizens for most of her history."

Gaea smiled. "We are neither separatists nor primitivists, nor do we intend to become what our ancestors were. The caravans in which we shall live and travel are large and as comfortable as any small starship, more comfortable by a great margin than the tiniest of them. They are fully equipped, and we will have both interstellar and surplanetary transceivers with us. Naturally, we shall have and maintain current tapes to ensure the proper education of our young.

"Every service we need will travel with us, and our own folk will eventually run the spaceport entirely, so there will be no need for those with a scientific or technical bent to emigrate to find desirable work.

"There will be no free birthing, of course, not even at this stage, and control will be as stringently kept once we reach population ideal as it is on Amon herself. Thus, we shall neither violate Jade nor create a situation where we have more hands than labor to occupy them."

"What do these grazers offer you?" Sogan asked her.

"Dairy goods since they are mammals, and fabric. I brought some samples of that last to show off."

With a pleased look the councilwoman handed them several swatches of finely woven cloth. Each piece was of a different color, ranging from pure white through all the browns and black plus a vivid yellow. All were soft, supple and appeared to be very warm.

"The yellow is from cows in breeding condition," Gaea explained. "In every case, the hair takes stripping and dying very well and lends itself to every form of working and tread formation we have tried thus far."

Her eyes glowed as she allowed them to see the importance of this subject to her and to her people.

"It is easy stuff to harvest, too. When the coat is ready to change, either in color or to thicken or lighten in response to the season, it just peels off, almost like the skin of a serpent or of some fruit. We need only collect it from rubbing rocks or bushes or take it ourselves from them when the creatures are tame enough. One or two good pulls should do it."

She sighed. "They have proven elusive subjects, though. They are peaceful, remarkably so, in fact, but they are quite unwilling to let us approach closer than a couple of yards. We have hesitated to try capturing any thus far for fear of turning them skittish or maybe stampeding the whole lot down on top of us. We are hoping the very young calves will give us a breakthrough when they are dropped next year."

Gaea sighed again. "Ah well, we have time, and we can still gather up the hair after it is shed."

"You will not export meat?" Sogan inquired.

The Councilwoman shook her head emphatically. "We wish to earn and be worthy of their trust. If we slaughtered them for others' use, we should be no more fit for that than if we of Amon took meat ourselves."

Islaen nodded, but she was frowning slightly. "The material is indeed fine and should soon be in good demand, but aren't you risking a lot in depending on one crop? A single disaster—"

Gaea shook her head. "We are not such fools, Colonel. There are many edible plants here, and every two families will share a garden caravan so that we shall never be in short supply. Beyond that, we have discovered that most of the flora produces either vegetable musk or ril oil, and in such quantity as to be readily harvested."

The Commando's brows raised. The former was one of the most valuable ingredients in the perfume industry, while the last, depending on how it was processed, was avidly sought either by the best chefs in the galaxy or as a lubricant for delicate-class and micro machinery.

"You seem to have found yourselves a generous world, Gaea of Amon," she said in admiration.

"There's more yet," Jake interrupted with an excitement apparent even without her talent for reading human emotion.

The older woman responded by emptying the contents of a small purse she had been holding onto a nearby table.

"Oh . . ." Islaen was not aware that gasp of pure rapture had escaped her as her fingers reached out to touch the glittering stones.

All were the clear blue-green of fine Terran aquamarines, but inside each one of them was a perfect frozen droplet, slightly deeper in shade than the surrounding jewel.

River Tears. They were among the galaxy's rarest and most valuable gems, having been found thus far on only two other planets in all the ultrasystem.

They were a fabulous resource for Jade's people, but at this stage of the colony's development, they might also pose a serious threat to its very survival, and the Commando was not surprised by the fleeting touch of concern she once again detected in Jake. It was well merited.

Such treasure could draw others with no right to it, and first-ship settlers lacked both the numbers and the resources to guard it adequately. If looters came too frequently or too violently, the Amonites might not be able to withstand the pressure at all.

"Would you like a Navy or Patrol guard stationed here?" she asked quietly.

Gaea shook her head. "No, not at this stage. We appreciate the danger of these gems as well as their value and have decided that neither we nor our children will reveal their presence on Jade. We have so informed our Settlement Agent and have instructed him to place all mention of the discovery under tight security classification. If this does not seem to be enough, we shall, of course, seek Federation aid, but we much prefer to stand on our own as far as and as soon as we can."

Islaen smiled. "That's most understandable, Councilwoman. Your precautions should be sufficient, and I do congratulate you on this find."

The older woman nodded her thanks. "Jakc informs me that you have leave time. If you are willing, you might spend a few days with us. We could then both offer you hospitality and at the same time show you something of what we have already accomplished in establishing ourselves on Jade."

"We'll be delighted to do so. Jake has your coordinates. As soon as we've finished up here, we'll fly out to your camp."

Her mind touched Sogan's.

She's proud of her baby. . . . she began quickly, knowing Gaea's offer would not please him; the Arcturian was never really comfortable in close association with others for any long period, even with these people who knew the secret of his race, and put no blame against him because of it.

Aye, his answer came swiftly, *and Jake is worried.*

You felt that, too?

She had kept her receptors linked with his as she usually did in any gathering so that he could share in the information she was receiving, but those touches had been so fleeting that she was not certain he had been able to detect them.

I did, and more strongly, your response to them. Have him ride with us if you can. He might talk to us more freely if he were alone in our company.

I'd intended it, Admiral.

SIX

JAKE KARMIKEL SETTLED himself in the rear seat of the Commando flier with a sigh of contentment. "This brings back memories. Are you going to open it up, Sogan?"

"No. We shall get there fast enough. No use in announcing her abilities to all and sundry."

"Well and good."

His eyes danced merrily. It was not difficult to guess that the former Admiral was in no particular hurry to reach the colonists' encampment. "Don't worry about your quarters. The Councilwoman's quite correct in her assessment of their comfort."

He favored his companions with a sudden, mischievous grin. "You might even consider this a second honeymoon. From what I hear, you had a few interruptions on the first one."

His tone changed abruptly. "Whipping a pirate armada with a handful of freighters . . ."

Sogan shrugged. "Freighters have had to do their own fighting for a long time. They are tough and well-armed, and there were a lot of good Navy veterans on-world to assure that they were adequately manned. Stark need and Islaen's rank were not long in wielding them into a respectable defense force."

"That would've meant little if we hadn't had a superb space

commander to lead it," the woman said gravely.

Sogan merely shrugged again. "I was annoyed. One of my caste is expected to endure a considerable amount of inconvenience, but a pirate invasion on my marriage night was rather beyond what I was prepared to tolerate."

He gave a soft laugh. "Maybe that is why most of your Resistance movements proved so unaccountably effective. Our coming must have disturbed many such an occasion."

Karmikel responded with an exaggerated shake of his head. Sogan had answered him as would a Commando, but there could be no slighting or passing off the incredible victory these two had gained between them or of the danger they had faced in the winning of it.

Jake made him no answer. He drifted into his own gloomy thoughts. It was vast and for the most part beautiful, this universe into which they had been born, and its planets and starlanes offered an almost infinite variety of lifestyles, enough to satisfy any individual or society.

Why was that not enough? Why could humankind and its equivalents not be content with all they had been given or which lay within their honorable ability to gain? Why must there ever be those who would slay and despoil, enslave and rob? Through all his youth and for all his manhood, he had known danger's shadow, be it far or near, and had fought that shadow, and there was a darkness on his heart in this moment which proclaimed that he should never in whatever remained of his life be completely free of it. Why must this be so? By the Spirit ruling all space, why must this blight ever ride his kind?

"Jake?" The Commando-Colonel's voice was soft, gentle, and he gave her a rueful smile.

"I'm glad you're here, especially you, Islaen."

"There's fear on you."

"Not that, not yet, but I am concerned."

His eyes met hers. "It's nothing concrete, and I haven't wanted to say anything to Gaea, but I was anxious for a chance to talk with you two, enough so that I should have asked you to come had you decided to cancel or delay this holiday."

"What's wrong?"

"What do you know about Thurston Sandstone?"

"Jade's Settlement Agent?" the Arcturian asked in surprise, speaking for the first time.

"Aye."

"Nothing much," the Colonel replied. "He has considerable experience, I understand, and is reputed to be thorough in his explorations and the preparation of his reports. I think I heard he's Terra-born, but I've had no reason to run a study on him. I shouldn't have bothered my head even this much about him if he weren't involved with the Amonites." Her eyes narrowed. "You apparently distrust him."

"In truth, I do, though I'm completely without any solid cause. It's more a gut reaction than anything."

"But there is something else?" she pressed.

He nodded. "His response when the Amonites scotched his plans for them by deciding to follow the goldbeasts instead of taming some few and crop farming. He was furious, to the point that he was scarcely able to restrain himself from flying into an open rage."

"A bureaucrat's annoyance?" suggested Sogan.

"Hardly, not to that degree, and inflexible types aren't hired for settlement work. Unique solutions are too often required for that. Besides, he's been at this a long time and should be well used to it. Sure, it's almost a joke throughout the Federation that the Settlement Board spends months and fortunes formulating complex scenarios only to have them overthrown in moments by potential colonists who prefer something simple and workable."

Jake's normally open features clouded. "I wish you'd been there, Islaen. Your reading might have told us a great deal about his real feelings."

"Aye," the woman agreed somewhat grimly. "I especially don't like having river tears mixed up in all this. They'll be a great resource later, but right now just too many people know about them between Board officials and scientists and the various exploratory and study crews. Any one of them could decide to make a grab for them, and there are those in plenty who'd be only too willing to help in return for a cut of the take."

"That's about the way I see it," Jake concurred.

"A report'll be expected from me and shouldn't arouse suspicion, even if anyone's monitoring our transmissons," she said thoughtfully. "Everyone knows a Commando will stay in touch with base even when on leave. I'll call on scramble from the camp and have a complete check done on Sandstone."

"Put the Navy or Patrol on standby as well," Sogan advised. "In strength. Looters could come in quietly and work quietly, but a quick, open raid might be more profitable for a big operation."

Both his companions nodded. Any attempt on the stones would almost certainly have to be large and complex, and those in charge of it were not likely to waste any time. They would order a major raid, annihilate the spaceport and probably the main settlement, clear out the stones, which were found in isolated, surface pockets, at their leisure, and vanish again before anyone could become aware of the attack, leaving no witnesses behind to describe it. That had happened all too often in the Federation's history, and it happened still, even now, when vastly improved communications and fast, efficient interstellar drive permitted far greater and closer vigilance. All of them might be acting the fool in this and wronging a good man besides, but the Amonites had already known too much of ill luck and treachery, and the potential for disaster was too clearly present here to be ignored. Each one of them would feel a great deal better with a strong force near at hand to stand guard.

The mood of the three lightened as they moved away from the flat country surrounding the spaceport and entered the hilly lands separating it from the broad river plain where the major portion of the Amonites were presently located. It was a fair land of gently rolling rises covered with a rich assortment of vegetation, sometimes waist high to a tall man.

There were no trees—Jade had produced none—but fine clusters of brush dotted the slopes, always in small, distinct stands most attractive to the eye. In no place on the planet did any equivalent of a forest or wood exist.

The sky was marvelous. It was deeply blue and was possessed of such cloud formations as took the very breath from Islaen. Rarely had she beheld anything like this. Offhand, she could think of but one place consistently displaying similar glory, the fair island in northern Terra where her own forebears had originated in the legendary past. She had visited there once after the close of the War and had been powerfully moved by its beauty and drama. Now, on Jade of Kuan Yin, she found something akin to it. The Amonites were indeed fortunate folk to have found such a world for their own.

She was not the only one to appreciate the planet's beauty and richness. The woman glanced at Varn. His expression was light, free, almost young. She could feel contentment and a quiet excitement on him and the flow of his power as he swept the world around them, seeking contact with Jade's animal life.

The Arcturian sensed her gaze on him and gave her a soft smile. He opened his mind to hers so that she might share in the readings he was receiving.

Islaen's face soon brightened in delight. Jade was indeed blessed with a rich fauna, and much of it, at least in this area, was of an intelligence high enough to support real, sustained curiosity. In their own way, the native creatures were welcoming and observing them even as Sogan was attempting to do.

She sighed in her own heart. How she envied her husband this gift! She could receive sendings only from her own species or those equivalent to it. Her experiences on Visnu and her contacts with Varn had sharpened her talent, allowing her to detect less intense, gentler radiations than she had previously been able to pick up, but still, so much of what she read was dark or violent and all too often openly evil. Subhuman transmissions could of a certainty be terrifying—Visnu had proven that all too graphically—but only those gifted with the so-called power of reason were moved by base considerations—the lust for blood, greed, the damning need to crush and enslave . . .

Islaen stopped herself. That was a grim train of thought, and she did not want Varn to pick it up. Moments such as this did not come often enough to him that she would willingly put any blight on him now.

Sogan did not slow or stop his vehicle during the journey, and at last they reached the final ripple of highlands overlooking the river plain.

The formation before them was unique, for the hill, though small, supported two distinct crests separated by a narrow depression, very like the horns of some mighty beast.

Sogan started to bring the flier through this miniature valley, but Jake leaned forward from his place in the rear.

"Go to the top, and let's get out for a while. The plain's well worth seeing from this vantage, and there aren't any ravagers here to make sight-seeing unpleasant."

"Predators?" the Colonel asked.

"Surprisingly few, all of them down below, stalking the herd."

"I could do to stretch my legs a bit," she conceded. "Varn can tell us if any wildlife with unacceptable interests should come sniffing around."

Karmikel nodded. He was one of the very few who knew of his companions' strange talents, the only one besides the Commando-Colonel to be aware of Sogan's. Islaen's gift had proven itself a thousand times over in the course of their harsh work during the War. The Arcturian's had awakened only lately, but he had seen something of it—enough, at least, to accept his former commander's assurance of its efficiency.

They left the flier well below the crest of the hill and walked to the top, glad of the exercise after the hours of confinement in the vehicle.

The scene before them was impressive in its own way although not nearly as fair as that behind.

A broad, extremely flat region lay below, so level that the perspective was similar to that of a more varied landscape seen from an altitude of several hundred feet. A vast darkness lay upon it. Animals, very large and almost without numbering.

"Goldbeasts?" the woman inquired.

Jake nodded. "Three-quarters of a billion of them, and a slightly greater number than that of gurries, though you can't see them from this distance."

"Gurries?"

He laughed. "I don't know where the Amonites got that name, but they're nothing at all like Noreen's brooding barnyard fowl. These are winged and feathered, right enough, but they're mammals, and the biggest of them don't quite reach nine ounces in weight."

Jake smiled. "They're cute little things. In fact, I think half our supposedly strictly serious-minded colonists are as much interested in acquiring some of them as pets as they are in taming the grazers."

"They must be proper little magicians to work that kind of conquest," Islaen remarked dryly. "Can you pick up anything from here, Varn?"

"Not much," he said, answering aloud for Jake's benefit although he had linked his mind with the woman's so that she received all that he did. "I can detect no individual touches, just a general sort of hum. There are two distinct species all right, both of them well contented and secure in themselves. If there are predators, their numbers are too few for me to detect."

He frowned suddenly, and Islaen felt a momentary puzzlement pass through him, but he shrugged it off and turned his attention to the river that had created all that great flatland.

It was clearly visible in the distance, a broad ribbon glittering like liquid gold under Kuan Yin's gentle rays.

"An impressive waterway."

"Aye," the other man agreed. "Even the miles can't take its size away from it. They do flatter it, though. It's very muddy up close."

Sogan glanced back over his shoulder. "There is some animal nearby."

"Aware of us?" the former Commando asked.

"No, I do not believe so." He frowned. "The readings are strange, somehow distorted. I cannot detect any specific interest or focus, yet there is a sort of overwhelming desire—"

"Don't worry about it, just so long as it doesn't seem likely to bother us." Jake turned back to the panorama below. "See that glinting away upstream? That's the camp. Kuan Yin's rays are reflecting off the caravan windows—"

"Quiet! Stand still!"

At Sogan's hissed warning, both his companions froze in place, their war-honed reflexes blocking any exclamation or start of surprise.

"To the left. Turn your heads slowly."

They obeyed.

A great creature stood on the rise's other horn. It was huge, a full twenty hands at the shoulder, coal black, and gaunt. The head was crudely triangular, hornless but covered with bony protuberances, especially obvious over the small, light-colored eyes, which were just barely visible at the distance separating them. The nose was very big and was a startling white.

"A goldbeast!" Karmikel exclaimed in surprise, keeping his voice low. "What's he doing here?"

"Do not move!" the former Admiral cautioned sharply. "He is mad. That is why I could not read him properly before. He scents us, and the hunger to bring death is on him."

"Our best bet would be to run for the flier," Islaen judged. "Our blasters could probably bring him down, but maybe not right away, and we'd have to let him get awfully close. —Can we make it if he starts to charge, Jake?"

"Perhaps. Goldbeasts can match a racing hound despite their size, and the distance is short. He's sure to come for us as soon as we move. . . ."

"Run!" Sogan ordered. "He is about to charge our scent!"

Even as they whirled, a clear belling roar rent the air. The enraged creature's forefeet struck the ground, not back towards him in the manner of a steer but forward, sending great clots of soil and pebbles out from him. They struck again, this time scything from right to left, felling the grass before him like a reaper of pre-space times.

The bull charged then, tearing downslope with the fearsome speed and unrelenting force of an avalanche, bugling loudly as he came.

All three off-worlders were in superb condition, but their lungs were heaving wildly by the time they reached their vehicle, short though the distance separating them from it had been.

The maddened goldbeast was almost upon them! They vaulted inside, mentally praising Kuan Yin for the pleasant heat which had induced them to keep the canopy drawn back. Had they been forced to open it, they would have had to fight.

Sogan's hand hit the vertical rise control even as he tumbled into the control seat. The flier shot into the air just as the bull ripped down upon them.

He gave a frenzied roar and reared up on his hind legs, slashing the air with his deadly hooves. His wrath was futile. The humans were away, free in Jade's sky where his mad hate could not reach them.

As soon as Sogan righted himself, he brought the Commando vehicle down a little and moved out onto the plain. Once he was certain they had passed the point where pursuit was likely, he slowed to their former rate of travel.

Jake sat back with an open sigh of relief. "Admiral," he said with feeling, "your talents are every bit as useful as the Colonel's here. I'm right glad you were around to pick up that reading, or we all might be pulp by now."

"Aye."

There was a tightness in that, and the Noreenan man looked sharply at him. "It was bad?" he asked.

"Worse than the ravagers," Islaen replied quietly for him.

Sogan nodded. "They slew mindlessly, but it was insatiable hunger that drove them, the need of so many individual things to feed. This other was possessed only of the lust to bring death." A visible shudder passed through him. "It is a diseased and debased touch to receive into one's mind."

"A renegade goldbeast," Karmikel mused after a moment's silence. "The idea seems particularly strange considering what mild, peaceful creatures they are. According to the presettlement studies, they don't even fight at mating time."

He frowned slightly. "You know, I think we saw them drive that fellow away. About three weeks ago, several dozen queen cows and bulls cornered a bull, actually encircled him, and herded him off toward the highlands. He was bugling mad like that one back there and slashing with his hooves, and a few took some good strokes back at him in return, but mostly, they just kept him moving.

"We were intensely curious, of course, but it all happened fast, and before we could do anything about following them, we found ourselves surrounded as well by several hundred animals. We were afraid of a stampede with the situation being so abnormal, so we merely tightened our caravan circle and stayed put.

"Everything had quieted down again in less than an hour and has been perfectly peaceful since."

"It is most strange," Sogan said, speaking softly, as if more to himself than to either of his companions.

"Aye, but first-shippers always have a great deal to learn about their new worlds, however thorough the Settlement Board has been."

"I suppose you are right," the Arcturian replied. "Let us hasten now. We still have a good distance to cover, and I am certain Gaea of Amon will be eager for a report of today's adventure. Forewarning of this danger could save lives at some future date."

It was early evening by the time the Commando vehicle drew near to the colonists' settlement, or camp, rather, since they had elected not to establish any permanent place for themselves.

Islaen felt disappointed in the site after her journey through the hill country, although it was hardly unattractive in itself, particularly to one who had herself been bred on a relatively flat planet like Noreen. The river plain had a kind of dingy look, but there was a quiet grandeur about it, a dignity, both restful and satisfying to the eye.

The waterway creating and dominating the scene was huge, awesome, ten miles in width in this place and broader still at its mouth over 1,700 miles to the south. It ran swiftly, carrying vast amounts of yellow sediment with it so that it had a deep dun color instead of the bright silver normal to flowing water. The liquid was potable in an emergency, she knew, but required processing to render it aesthetically acceptable under more normal circumstances.

The great bed was sunk deep in the rich soil, and rippling out from it on either side was a sea of lush grass and the clusters of brush and waist-tall herbs that represented the largest vegetable growth on Jade.

Upon this plain, stretching far beyond the limits of vision, grazed a nearly incomprehensible number of large, four-legged animals, the goldbeasts which were to shape the colonists' lives. Flying things, the tiny, feathered mammals which the Amonites had unaccountably called gurries, flitted around them or scratched upon the ground, pecking at the grain scattered in the mighty herd's feeding. Many were perched, apparently in the greatest ease and comfort, upon their huge companions' backs.

The newcomers were given little time to observe them further. As soon as their machine slowed to a stop, they were surrounded and enthusiastically escorted into the camp by the Amonite settlers, all of whom were eager to make them welcome and to show them the progress they had already made toward establishing themselves on Jade.

There was much to be seen and to say even without reporting the incident with the renegade bull, much to examine and study, and it was well after Kuan Yin's setting before the weary three were finally free to retire to the caravans reserved for their use.

Islaen Connor returned to the main room of the big wagon, which was designed to serve as an eating and general living area for its occupants.

She slowly sat on the long couch occupying most of one wall. Her hand unconsciously ran over its smooth cover. The material was bright yellow, warm and cheerful, nearly the color of a breeding goldbeast cow.

That brightness was a mockery to the feeling of gloom which had been growing within her almost since she had first arrived in the camp, poisoning her spirit until her heart seemed a leaden weight in her breast. She wearily pressed her fingers to her eyes. If only Jake's fears were wrong . . .

Varn saw and felt her sigh. He turned swiftly from the window where he had been standing and came to her. He sat beside her, covering her hand with his own.

Islaen, what trouble is on you? Is it Karmikel's suspicions?

She nodded. *Aye. Varn, I can't bear that this should be happening again! These people don't need more betrayal, more heartbreak. They deserve better . . .*

The pressure of his fingers increased until it was slightly painful, enough so as to draw her out of herself a little. *They may not be facing anything of the sort. That is for us to discover.*

The woman stared at him somewhat blankly for a moment, then suddenly the tension broke within her, and she smiled.

So we shall. I'll be heading over to the communications caravan in a few minutes, and we'll see what can be learned about this Thurston Sandstone of the Settlement Board.

The man is supposed to be experienced according to you and Jake, and his record is presumably good, or he would not have been given so publicized an assignment. What would move him to violate his trust now?—I still do not know your peoples' ways well enough to understand what drives such a one to treachery, he added, speaking stiffly, as he always did when admitting to what he considered to be some failing.

Our basic motives aren't very different from those moving the Empire's folk. As for Sandstone, if he is guilty, he may just never have been tempted seriously before. Those river tears are a rich prize, the more so since a pocket can be cleared out so easily and quickly. Just one success would set him and everyone in it with him up very, very nicely for the remainder of their lives. Think about it. One risk, only one, and he need never chance himself again.

You think that might be the answer?

She shook her head. *I don't know, Varn. The Federation tries to choose candidates of high character for such positions, but no system is infallible, and people do change with time. One thing for certain, I'm going to ask that criminal scenarios be run, and aberration scenarios as well. I'm not going to take a chance with just a straight biographical study, not in this.*

Aberration?

Sogan's face tightened and more so the pattern of his thoughts. It had been his own commander's undiagnosed insanity that had forced the decision on him which had cost him his place within the Empire and very nearly his life.

Aye, the Commando answered, carefully schooling herself to seem unaware of his reaction. *We could find our motive there when a search for a logical one might come up blank.*

Will you be able to get the information you want? Your Federation boasts that it respects its citizens' rights to privacy and freedom from official hounding.

Sandstone isn't a private citizen. All public officials know that a certain amount of scrutiny comes with the job. Otherwise, the potential for corruption would be too great. Besides, it's not that he'll be dragged before the Patrol or a psychomedic. You know full well that scenarios are strictly possibility studies, courses suggested by the combining of a variety of potential and real factors based on what we know and can learn of the subject. They're no confirmation of guilt, but they can sure as hell point the way for further investigation.

Aye, and they are also difficult and very costly procedures. Will your request be sufficient to move your people into doing what you want done? We were not sent here on any investigation, after all.

They'll be done. Admiral Sithe'll see to that. He handpicked his senior Commando officers, and he has enough trust in us to respond when one of us says there's a need for some action.

He would be a fool if he did not if your comrades are anything the likes of you, Islaen Connor.

Her eyes sparkled. *That's blatant flattery, Admiral Sogan.*

The man smiled. *Perhaps, though I have found that works only when it is also true.*

It's good for the morale now and then, at any rate. The smile left her. *Thanks, Varn. You pulled me out of that hole I was in.*

You were tired, and the possibility of this trouble came as an unpleasant surprise. Then, too—

His thought broke off, and his eyes drew away from hers.

She looked at him in surprise. *Then, too, what?*

I have no right—

Rot! A lot of lives may be hanging on us right now. I also happen to be your wife. If we can't talk to each other—

Very well, he said reluctantly, then he faced her again. *You are too involved with these people. You identify too strongly with them, and they have come to mean too much to you for you to consider anything affecting their welfare dispassionately.*

For one instant, her brown eyes flashed fire, but after that, her anger cooled. *You're right,* the guerrilla admitted. *You think I should ask for someone else to take over on Jade?*

No. No, I do not. I considered that, but the Spirit of Space seems to have willed this on us. We shall have to begin it, and it is rarely wise to change officers in the midst of a campaign, even if the Amonites would readily accept anyone else's lead.

That Jade's settlers were not likely to do, she thought, particularly if they had been betrayed by a Federation official. They were none too trusting of outside influence or control as it was.

What are you suggesting, then?

Only that you take great care in this, that you be sure your mind and warrior's instincts rule you and not your emotions.

I will. Have no fear of that.

She smiled a bit tightly. *I owe you one for that warning, Comrade. Wait for me here. I want this transmission to seem nothing more than a normal check-in, and you wouldn't bother coming with me for that. I won't be too long.*

Varn Tarl Sogan slipped into the sleeping area of the big wagon, a small but adequate cubicle set above and nominally warmed by the drive mechanism, which never completely shut down.

Islaen had gone up before him since he had told her he wanted to think alone for a while, and now his somewhat harsh features softened as he gazed down upon her.

She was already asleep. Her lovely face looked relaxed and peaceful nestled there amidst the heavy blankets needed to combat Jade's night chill.

He held very still so that no sound should disturb her and set tight shields on his mind. Seeing her like this put a heaviness on his spirit that he did not want to reach her.

The former Admiral remembered how his consort's great eyes had widened when Gaea of Amon had spilled out those river tears for them to examine. She had not lusted for them, but she had loved them, and Islaen Connor was a woman worthy of possessing and wearing such beauty. She was worthier by far in person and loveliness than any of the fair residents in the Emperor's own harem.

Sogan's face hardened once more. It burned him, shamed him, that he who once, on a mere impulse, could have bought the entire contents of the Councilwoman's purse could not now so much as dream of ever acquiring the smallest part of any such treasure for his own wife's delight.

He sat beside the sleeper, carefully so as not to jostle the bed. This marvelous woman had given him so much, and he had profited beyond all imagining from the connection she had established for him with the Commandos and the Federation Navy, yet he himself had returned so little as to amount to nothing. . . .

As gently as he had moved, the Commando's eyes flew open. They brightened in welcome at the sight of him, and his own warmed in response.

I did not mean to wake you.

No matter, she murmured sleepily. *It's cold. Aren't you ready to call it a day yet?*

I am.

His consort sat up, keeping the blankets wrapped about herself to ward off the chill.

Hurry, then, she said with a smile. *Remember what Jake said we should consider this trip!*

He bent to kiss her. *I am not about to forget it, my Islaen.*

SEVEN

ISLAEN MOVED BRISKLY away from the encampment. It was still very early, and the air had a bitter bite to it so that she huddled in upon herself, instinctively making herself small inside her service jacket. It seemed like all the world around her was asleep. None of the settlers had risen as yet, and even the grazers and their winged companions were but dark lumps upon the ground.

She paused a moment to watch them. Her look was wary. Despite the fact that the creatures were showing themselves to be fully as placid as the Board's studies told them to be, she was none too happy about wandering alone like this in their midst after her experience with the renegade bull, and she resolved to take good care not to come too near any of the tightly massed pods into which they divided themselves.

Goldbeasts were creatures demanding respect. They were big, many of them even larger than the one which had attacked them, and the hooves crowning their multijointed forelegs were sharp as knives. They might indeed use them chiefly to dig out succulent roots in the southland where grasses were less prominent in the floral mix and to aid in finding and holding purchase on the steep highland tracks they sometimes followed, but she thought it would be a daring predator who would spring at a wary cow or bull. At any rate, she had no intention of inadvertently issuing any challenges or alarms.

The woman's care did not lessen her interest in the huge animals.

Goldbeasts were almost amazingly ugly with big, lumpy faces, pale eyes, and enormous white noses, but it was that kind of ugliness which rather tended to arouse affection than distaste. They certainly inspired no sensation of revulsion at all.

Their social organization was one fairly common to herd-dwelling wildlife throughout the Federation. The big herd was comprised of individual pods consisting of about a dozen adult cows plus their immature offspring. The bulls roamed freely among them, either singly or in small groups of up to four animals.

There was little competition amongst these males and almost no conflict. Most of the relatively few bull calves were dropped in the north just before the start of the long southward migration, and only the strongest of them survived to reach these fields of plenty and rest, where they immediately became prime targets for predators until the multitude of females were delivered shortly after the herd's arrival, finally relieving the pressure on them. Thus, only the fleetest and most able males survived to maintain the species, rendering the need for turbulence and squandered energies at mating time all but unnecessary.

The woman did not delay long watching the beasts once she reassured herself that she had not disturbed them and that none of them would take undue interest in her. Sogan had gone out even earlier than she. Something had been puzzling him, and he had wanted to resolve it, or at least to clarify it more in his own mind, before discussing it with her. Now, he had reached some conclusion, and he had called to her, waking her and asking her to meet him by the river.

She shivered as the wind whipped around her and rather irritably wished that he had merely told her what he wanted instead of rousting her out of her blankets, too.

She quelled her sour feelings in the next instant lest he read them. Although they were now so accustomed to this linking of thought that they could in fact converse at considerable distance if need demanded it, both still found it easier and more comfortable to talk while in one another's actual presence, within normal verbal conversational range.

They spotted each other in about the same instant, and Islaen felt the exultant surge of joy with which he always greeted her.

She gave him welcome, glorying in the happiness she brought him and in the marvelous warmth of mind and heart that was so sharp a contrast to the cool reserve with which he bore himself when in the presence of others.

The woman's pace quickened to a run, but an alarmed squawk brought her to a halt before she had gone more than a couple of yards.

She glanced down to see a tiny brown form sprawled at her feet. A young gurry. She had not seen her in the dim, post-dawn light and had very nearly walked on her.

The little hen-chick seemed to radiate terror, and the Commando-Colonel scooped her up, cuddling and warming her in her hands. "You poor little darling," she murmured soothingly. "I won't hurt you. I'd never in all my life harm anyone like you, not for all the glories of the ultrasystem."

You should be hard pressed to do so, you or anyone else worthy of being called human.

Sogan had come up beside her. He stroked the small head with his forefinger. *These gurries see to that very efficiently.*

Islaen stared at him and then at the chick. *Influence?* she asked. *Mental influence?*

Very definitely. I suspected something from my readings yesterday, but my impressions were so mixed that I wanted to work them out a little before sharing them with you.

He rubbed the young hen's head once more. This time, she uttered a sound that was half-whistle, half-purr.

There is nothing sinister involved. Our feathered friends merely project goodwill in large doses. Nothing with any significantly measurable intelligence has the slightest desire to do them injury. Even most of Jade's predators do not trouble them apparently, just a few amphibians that take chicks before they manage to attach themselves to one of the goldbeasts, who thereafter provide ample protection. This one has not found herself a partner yet, or she would have been snuggled up with it, nice and warm for herself, instead of roosting on the ground.

The woman looked at him sharply. *You've been able to read so much?*

Of course not, though I did learn more than I normally can from them. Their touch is more like communication than that of any other animal I have encountered. Some of my surmises come from what we have learned since arriving here and from the Board reports I read last night, the rest from reasoning and deduction. I may not be entirely correct on every point, but I think I have most of it right.

His earlier words had sharpened Islaen's awareness of the chill, and she drew her hands closer to her body.

There was no sign of fear on the gurry now. She nestled more comfortably into the human's hands with a distinct air of satisfaction and lifted her face to gaze curiously at them.

The Commando laughed. The hen-chick was a merry, mischievous-looking little thing with black, extraordinarily bright eyes peering out from a stripe of dark feathers that circled her head like the mask of a pre-space Terran thief. The semiflexible bill was a bright yellow and was curled up in what appeared to be a smile of utter contentment.

"Why you little bandit!" Islaen exclaimed, shifting her hold enough so that she might free her fingers to stroke the chick. "I think I don't care if you are instigating it all. I still love you."

She glanced at her companion. *It's true, you know. I should like such a creature, influence or not. As Jake said, gurries are cute.*

Sogan nodded, smiling. Islaen was drawn to an astonishingly broad spectrum of creatures, but she was correct about this one. The small mammal was singularly appealing.

They do have the advantage of being attractive to humans. No one, at least no one currently on Jade, would want to harm them.

You've made some discovery, Varn.

A partial discovery only. I wish I could figure—

Nooo!

Both froze, then turned to face one another. That cry had not sounded in their ears but was a moan of pure distress ringing in their minds.

The chick was whimpering piteously and struggling to cling to Islaen's hands with her amazingly supple toes, fighting her efforts to return her to the ground.

The woman quickly straightened again. "Where do you want to go, then, Bandit?" The small animal took wing in answer and perched upon her shoulder.

Sogan chuckled. *It looks like she has found herself the*

equivalent of a goldbeast. Actually, you are fortunate. She might have decided to settle upon your head.

Very funny!

The Arcturian grew serious once more, but his eyes were glowing with excitement. *Bandit has answered my remaining questions for me, I think. Listen.*

So saying, he linked his receptors with hers. Now, sensations filled Islaen's mind, indescribably alien and emanating from sources well-nigh without finite number.

The woman was accustomed to this sharing of perception by then and so did not recoil or freeze but rather reached out eagerly to experience and understand the strange contacts.

After a few moments, her brows came together. There was something different here, something very different. She had read herd creatures before, but the experience had not been like this.

Her eyes fixed on Varn in wonder.

Information flowed through the vast multitude. Each grazer was in full contact with every other and with the flying things which accompanied them. It was not speech in the human sense, but there was interchange and interaction, and it was both conscious and in well-nigh continuous operation.

The gurries! she whispered.

He nodded. *They are the catalysts. I knew the goldbeasts do not have the capability for accomplishing this by themselves, not on this scale, whatever their individual intelligence, and I did not understand how it could be happening until Bandit told us by her adoption of you.*

What are we going to do?

That must be your decision, Sogan told her gravely.

He was right, of course. By her orders, Commando-Colonel Islaen Connor was not merely a Federation troubleshooter but both a diplomat and a senior official as well. Authority and its inherent responsibility were hers.

The Amonites should be told. They must be told. Full knowledge of their new homeworld was their right, but she was very loath to reveal the method by which they had made their discovery. Jake knew of the power they shared, but neither she nor Varn Tarl Sogan would voluntarily permit any other to learn of it. Neither of them had any desire to pass the remainder of their lives as laboratory specimens for the Federation's scientists.

Let me think on it, she said slowly. *At worst, we can claim we reasoned it out, but if we can get a few gurries adopted, and they can communicate with the others as Bandit does with us, then we're away with it.*

She bent a soft smile upon the chick, her affection calling forth a veritable storm of purring. *Sure, once the others see her with me, everyone'll want one even if they didn't before.*

We shall soon find out, the man remarked, pointing toward the camp.

A youth or very young man was hastening in the direction of one of the nearer pods, a blanket of yellow goldbeast hair clasped about his shoulders to ward off the chill.

Sogan's lips curved into a smile. Their arrival the previous day and the news of their adventure had sparked a late night, and the lad must have wakened somewhat after his time. The work of trying to tame at least a few of the pods, if only to the point of accepting human presence at close range, was in full though thus-far-unsuccessful swing, and no duty-conscious Amonite would delay for something as trivial as proper dress or his own comfort.

All of a sudden, a high, clear bugling tore the stillness of the morning apart. A bull! He was not mad, this one, but the mating fires waxed hot within him.

The mighty black called once more, then, with all the irresistible force of a planetbuster, he charged the horror-frozen boy.

Islaen's hand went for her blaster, but the distance was too great, and the bolt struck far short. Sogan's fell equally without effect.

You scramble-circuited vacuum brain! That is no cow!

No sooner had the desperate thought burst from his mind than the goldbeast broke his charge, halting so abruptly that he slid back onto his haunches.

Oh.

Disappointment and puzzlement poured into them, and into the Amonite boy as well, they saw. He was standing frozen in place, one hand covering his open mouth, too amazed in that moment to realize or care how utterly comical he appeared.

Their astonishment ended, transmuted into concern. The bull straightened himself but seemed to be favoring one of his legs.

"You're hurt!" Islaen cried, broadcasting in mind as well as speech. "Let me see if I can't help!"

The huge creature stood still, watching her curiously as she approached. He made no effort to move away from her.

The Arcturian's heart beat fast. He hastened to the Amonite. "Take that blanket off," he ordered once he was near enough to make himself easily heard. "Bring it over and show him what it is."

"But-but he is angry," the other protested, anxiously eyeing the great muscles and wicked-looking hooves.

Sogan studied him, trying to gauge his age. "You would not be pleased with some lad who tricked you into thinking he was a lass."

The Amonite reddened a little and then grinned.

"No, I would not for a fact."

"Come on. Let him have a look at your blanket and explain what happened. Think your words as you speak them."

"Apologize to an animal?" he asked in wonder.

"Why not? You felt *his* dismay and found it comprehensible, and he did break his run at some inconvenience to himself when he might more easily have taken his frustration out on you."

The youth was frowning deeply. He did not want to argue with the off-worlder, but something most strange had happened here, and the more he thought on it, the more incredible it all became.

"How, by all Amon's great gods, can he understand me or I him?"

"Bandit, our gurry, makes it possible. —Lad, this is the breakthrough your people have been looking for with these grazers. Jump to claim it."

The boy squared his shoulders. Moving steadily and slowly so as not to startle the bull, he began walking toward him.

"I am sorry, Big One. I hope you are not hurt—"

"He's not," Islaen told him quickly. "Keep it up. He seems to like the attention."

"I did not mean to bother you. Really, I did not. See, it is only a blanket to keep me warm. I never thought it would cause you trouble."

The bull sniffed the cloth. He shook his head. Yellow hair meant a receptive cow. . . .

He is only a calf. Sogan's mind broadcast that in sudden inspiration. Even from the little he had seen and read and from the contacts he had established, it was apparent that in the herd's eyes, immature goldbeasts could do little wrong. Would the big creatures be able to carry the concept over to the human newcomers as well?

In a moment, he relaxed. The huge black nuzzled the boy, then licked his hand with a long, rough tongue.

"He likes me!" the Amonite murmured in a mixture of awe and delight that was nearly rapture.

Islaen's eyes fixed on her mate. *That was brilliant, Admiral,* her mind said.

He gave her a smile. *It might be best not to tell the lad about it.*

He glanced toward the encampment. The others were awake now, and they had been spotted. Nearly everyone was watching them, their excitement patent as they saw the boy stroking the erstwhile elusive grazer.

"Let us go back to your people," he said aloud, "and bring our native-born companions with us. We have meat here for a council."

EIGHT

THE COLONY'S DIRECTING Council with Gaea of Amon at its head was assembled in the center of the encampment, while the remainder of the populace was gathered around, each person pressing as closely as possible to hear what was being said.

The off-worlders were sitting beside the settlement leaders, as was Telly, the young herdsman.

Sogan smiled as he watched him stroke the bull, whom he had named Midnight. The boy's head was down, for he felt strange at being included in this gathering, but every now and then, he would glance at his agemates in the encircling crowd to see their wondering, envious glances.

He was wrapped in glory. Everyone might soon be dealing freely with the grazers, but it was obvious from every look he bent upon the goldbeast bull beside him that he could not even conceive of another nearly as fine or as brilliant as this black.

The Arcturian turned his attention back to the gathering. Islaen had finished delivering their startling news, following the story they had worked out between them on their way back to the settlement in which they let reasoning, the adoption of the gurry, and the incident with the bull account for his discovery, omitting completely the part his talent had played.

The first flurry of excited comment and question was ended, checked by the command of the Council members, and the

Commando-Colonel raised her hand for silence so that she might continue.

"I'd say that your next move would be to adopt gurries for yourselves. Luck's with you in the timing. The chicks are out of their nests and are well able to care for themselves, and there are still a goodly number of them who haven't paired off with goldbeasts yet. Some of you, at least, should be able to find partners without much trouble, and the rest can claim them next year."

"They seem to be affectionate little things, and they certainly are likeable," Gaea said, looking rather longingly at Bandit, who was preening herself and purring happily on Islaen's lap. "They are long-lived, too, according to the Settlement Board's studies, and so would make excellent companions, but I do not like the idea of accidentally harming them in some way through our ignorance of their needs."

"That should not happen," Sogan told her. "As Islaen mentioned, they can care for themselves, and partnership with larger creatures is their natural lifeway. They seem to be opportunistic," he added, "and more than willing to let humans provide whatever they require."

Amen, the Colonel's thought replied with no little feeling, but she only nodded gravely and said aloud, "Try with a few of them, using warm, responsible people to make the test. One thing for sure, communication with the herd appears to be dependent upon a personal relationship with gurries, although it seems that only one so tied need be present to permit interaction among several creatures."

Suddenly, her eyes flashed, and her tone altered so that both the Amonites and Sogan looked at her in surprise.

"It is interaction, too. That bull willed not to hurt Telly, and he willed to give his friendship only after an acceptable explanation of what had happened was made. Those goldbeasts may not be able to reason as would a human or work with complex abstract concepts, but they are possessed of both mind and feeling, and so are the gurries to an even greater degree."

"We are not likely to forget that," Gaea told her quietly. "We wish to share Jade's life, not be tyrants over it. We hardly expected anything like this, but I think I am one with all my people both in welcoming such a relationship and in my excitement over it."

An instantaneous murmur of assent affirmed her words. Islaen nodded her acceptance of that assurance.

"I'm glad to hear that. These little ones seem to hunger for love almost as other things do for food, and Midnight proves the grazers respond to kindness and fair dealing."

"They shall have both. I believe we can make an arrangement favorable to each species. Goldbeast hair is at its prime when it is being shed, and they should be pleased to have us relieve them of its weight quickly. In return, we can seek milk from them as well. There will never be so many of us that we would strain their own needs with our demands for it."

She smiled at Islaen's chick. "As for gurries, such winsome little things would not be long in captivating us even if they had no particularly useful talents. They were well on the way to that already. After seeing Bandit, I confess I should give much that I value to have someone look upon me with such devotion."

Sogan's dark eyes sparkled to hear that from the usually grave Councilwoman. His mind touched his consort's. *Do not fear for them, Colonel. Our feathered comrades will secure themselves very satisfactorily.*

So I see. —Why didn't they move sooner?

A soft touch sought entry into her mind.

Go ahead, Love, she invited in surprise.

Chicks were very small and frightened when humans came. You were strange. Too noisy. Mindways like predators'.

The impressions came clearly, although it was apparent to the stunned woman that only she and Sogan had received them.

She stroked Bandit with hands she was scarcely able to keep from trembling visibly. This was no mere beast that she held.

You're right, Small One, she replied, fighting to answer clearly despite the shock she had just received. *We humans are predators, and it's sometimes necessary to choose the kind from the harsh among us.*

She did not know how much of that thought the little creature understood, but the truth of it put a heaviness on her own spirit.

"The decisions must be yours, Councilwoman," she said aloud, "but for my part, I'd advise you to keep quiet about all you've learned today. Build on it and see what may develop out of it to be Jade's heritage."

"I was going to ask for your silence," the other responded promptly. "We want no interference with this. If for no other reason, Amonites hate bureaucracy, and we want no part of the committees and study teams word of such a relationship would inevitably draw down on us."

She looked somberly upon the Commando's gurry. "In truth, I should not be quick to permit anyone to cart these little ones off to their labs, terrifying them at the very least. They are Jade's, and if we are ever to be Jadites ourselves, it is surely ours to shield them as we would our own selves."

Varn Tarl Sogan quietly withdrew from the Amonite camp. Evening was well on now, and he judged he could at last seek a little time to himself without giving hurt or offense. There was certainly enough talk and excitement that the brief absence of one person should pass quite unnoticed.

The empty crates which had once housed parts of the big caravans had been pressed into service to strengthen the perimeter of the area the humans had temporarily claimed for their use. He sat upon one of these and took several deep breaths of the chilly air, feeling relieved to be away from the others and alone for a while.

He did not call to Islaen, knowing she would come out to him if he did so.

The former Admiral would have welcomed her company, but he knew she enjoyed these settlers, although Noreen had given rise to a merry race and Amon to a rather solemn one. She had a powerful respect for their courage and tenacity, and the agrarian cultures of both worlds made for a strong bonding and understanding between them.

He did not and could not share in that last, though he surely had an equal admiration for the Amonites' spirit and strength of purpose. He had been bred and schooled a war prince in an ultrasystem where all other castes counted as naught, and he could not now be entirely comfortable treating as an equal with those who were not warriors.

Sogan gave a bitter inner laugh, mocking himself. There were few with whom he dared be comfortable, as the incident on Horus all too clearly illustrated. An outcast from his own, he must ever remain a wanderer amidst potential foes . . .

He quelled the rush of self-pity threatening to overwhelm him. It was cowardice in itself and an enemy both to him and to the life he was trying to build. He smiled suddenly, tenderly. The life Islaen was helping him build.

The Arcturian turned away from the lighted area to face the vast darkness beyond and opened his mind to all he should find there.

As much excitement as there was in the human camp, that much and more again rippled through the wild things of Jade.

The most powerful readings were emanating from the gurries, he realized, from the as-yet-unclaimed chicks. Bandit had given report, and these others longed unutterably for even a small part of what she had gained.

Take care, he cautioned, certain his thoughts would reach their targets clearly between his own talent and Islaen's and his relationship with Bandit. *Islaen is one by herself. Not all humans are like her.*

Disappointment, so wrenching and deep that tears sprang to his eyes, poured into him, and he considerably altered his estimate of the flying creatures' intelligence scale. Much spiritual depth was required to anticipate so keenly and to mourn so sharply.

No, Little Ones. A great deal is possible, but take care with whom and how you share your lives. Some of my kind are harsh and cruel, though none of that lot should be here.

Could they understand that?

He received images, impressions, of bulls and, rarer still, of cows driven out from the herd, renegades acceptable to no pod, sought by no gurry, because a contempt for life tainted their hearts and fouled their deeds, creatures mad with blood lust and doomed to wander alone in the highlands or fall to former herdmates if they returned in the hope of slaying.

The man gently withdrew from the contact, leaving behind him his wish for their success. These gurries were wise, and he felt he could trust them to choose well.

Their touch had been pleasant, and he was still smiling in remembrance of it when he saw another man leave the camp and come toward him. Jake Karmikel. There was no mistaking the tall former Commando's walk.

He knew he was seen and raised his hand in greeting.

"Sit," he said when Karmikel drew close. "Did you get tired of questions at last?"

"Tired of being ignored, you mean. It's Islaen that everyone wants tonight. That was some coup you two pulled off."

"Thank Bandit for it, and that rather overeager bull."

The other man laughed. "They're a pair between them! I'm not all that fond of goldbeasts myself, but I don't mind admitting I wouldn't object to having a gurry around."

"Bandit pleads their case well," the Arcturian agreed; he and Islaen had decided to remain silent about the little mammals' ability to influence others in their favor lest it frighten the settlers off. They would learn about that soon enough on their own.

"You'll be keeping her?"

"Aye, if the Amonites do not object. She accepts our food, and Islaen would be heartbroken to leave her behind."

Jake managed not to smile. The Colonel was patently not alone in feeling affection for the Jadite creature.

"They're not likely to refuse you that. Right now, they've just about decided that the pair of you are a direct gift to them from Amon's ancient gods." He bent a wicked grin upon the other. "In fact, I shouldn't be surprised if there weren't altars being raised to you in another four or five hundred years."

"Let them make history tapes now!"

Jake chuckled. Noreen's gods were a gentle lot, enjoying their worshipers and taking amusement from them, but those of the Empire were cruel and hard, intolerant of any supposed attempt to usurp even the lightest of their privileges.

Sogan glowered at him, knowing he had been properly baited. "All Noreen's offspring are somewhat mad," he muttered sourly.

"That we are, friend."

Karmikel grew grave again. The former Admiral did not seem heavily pressed, yet he had withdrawn from the gathering and had remained apart some time now.

"Everything's all right? I saw you come out here—"

"Aye." Sogan shrugged. "There is that in me which has little liking for crowds. I intended no insult."

"It's called survival instinct, Comrade," the ex-Commando replied, relieved, "and you managed your departure well. I just chanced to see you go."

Karmikel frowned. "Islaen told me what happened on Horus. That could've been nasty."

"I have had to talk or fight my way out of such situations before," he replied a bit stiffly, as the memory of the fear he had felt for his wife returned to him.

The other man was silent for several seconds. "She looks good," he said suddenly.

"Islaen? Aye, our lifeway does agree with her."

Jake faced him. "She's happy. I had to know you were giving her that."

A sense of shame, of futility, filled Sogan. He wanted to turn from his companion, this one who had served long with Islaen Connor and had loved her long and who had possessed the manhood to step back when he saw how things must be.

Give? He made no return for what he received. The Colonel's use of the *Fairest Maid* could not stand against his debt to her, the most particularly not with the outfitting the starship had received. The much-increased threat to his own life was meaningless. His existence was nothing in itself, and he would be in some measure of peril whatever he did.

He was not about to make a show of his frustration and bruised pride, however, and he straightened, as if casually.

"It would be a poor man who would not try to keep her so. —Any word from Horus yet?"

He asked that merely to move them away from the uncomfortable topic since he did not believe any response to be possible in so short a time.

To his surprise, the Noreenan nodded. "Aye. Admiral Sithe moves fast when Islaen asks for something. He knows she doesn't cry wolf unless it's at the door."

"Well?"

"On the surface, it looks like I should reprogram my navputer. I seem to be flying right out of the galaxy.

"Thurston Sandstone has twenty-eight years of exemplary public service behind him. Because genetic testing showed the possibility of cardiac problems developing under conditions of prolonged, severe stress, he was asked to enter alternate civilian training instead of the military when he tried to enlist. He chose settlement work and proved so apt a pupil that he graduated with high ratings a full year before his entry-level classmates.

"He rose very rapidly within the Board as well, reaching his present position of Settlement Agent after only ten years. Since then, he's closed the files on seven colonies, all low-tech, low-impact settlements requiring no extensive adaptations. All seven are flourishing, and the first three have already established interstellar trade and are beginning to show a slight profit. Jade's his eighth planet and the only one to receive any extradepartmental publicity."

"What about the man himself?"

"There's precious little to tell. He's never married or openly taken a mistress, and if there were any more temporary affairs, he conducted them most circumspectly. There are no offspring, of course, and no close kin left."

"The War took them?"

Jake shook his head. "No, just normal attrition. He was an only child of a late marriage and spent his youth on Terra. The fighting didn't touch him."

"You mentioned he has no close kin. There are others?"

"Cousins, all well out, none of whom are in contact with him. There don't seem to be any close friendships either, although he has acquaintances in plenty and sees a number of business associates socially. It's not an unusual pattern, particularly among veterans in the various service professions."

"What about his personal habits?"

"No danger vices. No vices or quirks at all that we can discover. He lives quietly and in keeping with his position and means. Like many inner-system natives, Sandstone has rarefied and rather expensive tastes with respect to his possessions, and when he does indulge them, it's usually to acquire a piece of some importance and cost, but he does so only rarely, never going beyond the range of his salary or putting himself into debt or drawing from his retirement funds."

Karmikel sighed. "He doesn't sound like a serpent who'd rob a bunch of colonists depending on him, does he?"

"No, but is he capable of doing it?"

"That I don't know. Certainly, he has the brains to engineer a raid and to cover himself while doing it, and he probably has access to most or all the information and contacts he'd need if he were willing to do a bit of work."

"Could a man like he seems to be find the right personnel?"

"Not readily, perhaps, but if he were careful and persistent, aye, he could. If you wait long enough, you can find just about anything on Set."

That was true enough. Isis' fourth planet was a hole. She had no trade worth mentioning apart from her position as a major base for civilian governmental activities in the Sector, and her leaders chose to keep her port completely open. Those capitalizing on that freedom of entry realized they would be able to avail themselves of it only so long as they kept quiet and attracted little official attention, but it was well known that many a dark charter was picked up there.

Jake frowned. "The question is, would he?"

"Why should he after so long?"

"Who knows? He could be angry because others found glory while he was denied the opportunity to try for it, or he might feel bitter over his stagnated career, especially after his initial meteoric rise. He's tried before to move out of settlement work or farther up within the Board, but someone else has always been preferred over him for the places he's considered.

"It could also be plain greed. It must be hard for one of refined taste to constantly be forced to walk away from the things he wants. Surroundings are important to a man who's essentially alone like him, and Sandstone must realize that Federation work won't ever give him much more than he has now."

An ugly, chill finger seemed to run through Sogan as he recalled his own earlier thoughts, and he was glad it was Jake Karmikel and not his consort here with him. At least, this rush of guilt would not be betrayed.

"There must be many in a similar situation who regret and even resent it," he said carefully.

"They're legion, friend, and an awful lot of them are in a position to rectify things a bit, though few of them on anything like this scale, of course. Most of them wouldn't even dream of acting on their opportunity, or at least not of yielding to the temptation."

"Would Sandstone?"

"I don't know. I just don't know! Most of the scenarios came out negative. A clean robbery's just barely possible, but violence, and maybe a great deal of it, almost certainly has to be part of any move against Jade's stones. Every study agrees that he could be party to that only if he were laboring under such a weight of hatred or anger as to defy imagination."

"A massive aberration could give rise to that, particularly if coupled with some real or imagined other needs."

"Aye. Further tests are being run to try to determine if anything like that could be at work here, but it's pretty obvious the Navy thinks we're way off on this. Maybe they're right, but I felt there was something decidedly wrong about him, and I still do."

He sighed. "You can see it all for yourself when you go back to your caravan. I left the report there. Islaen can decide whether she wants to go on with it when she reads the thing."

His discouragement was apparent, and Sogan gave him a tight smile. "She will go on. She trusts in your instincts and, for whatever it is worth, so do I. You Commandos would not have stayed alive for long had you been unable to judge people. I very much doubt you have lost that ability merely because you have gone back into civilian life."

NINE

ISLAEN GLARED AT the chessboard. She was losing badly as usual, and Jake was enjoying the prospect of her imminent defeat thoroughly. He gave a crow of delight as he swept away her second knight.

"I could never understand, Colonel," he remarked conversationally, "how someone who plays this poorly ever had any success at all in penetration work."

"Just continue with the massacre, please," she replied with mock irritation. "Any more comments, and I'll refuse to feed your ego by playing the next time you suggest it."

Her interest in the game vanished suddenly. Bandit had been feeding with her own kind, but now, the gurry chick streaked through the open door of the caravan. Her feathers were extended to the full, and she squawked excitedly as she settled on the board, scattering several pieces apparently without noticing that she had done so.

"Love, what's wrong?" the woman asked in some alarm.

Renegade! Hates humans. Coming to kill, and goldbeasts must. Don't like. Humans do.

All that burst into Islaen's mind in one quick flood, and more would have followed fast upon it had she not interrupted.

"Hold up! You're going too fast, Love. Can it wait until

Varn comes? Together, we could probably understand you better."

Yes. Wait for Varn.

"Good. I'll call him. You just collect yourself and think out what you want to tell us. He's in our caravan and should be here soon."

Sogan came quickly in response to his consort's summons.

He turned at once to the gurry. "What has happened to upset you, Small One?" he asked gently. "You seem very much disturbed."

"You should have seen her when she arrived," Jake told him.

"Never mind that," Islaen said. "Go on, Bandit."

With their minds linked so that they might fully utilize both the Arcturian's talent and the Noreenan woman's tie with the hen, they soon had her story. This, they then relayed to Jake.

All three sat grim-faced and silent for several minutes, then the Commando-Colonel shook her head. "I'm not going to give an answer to this on my own authority. It's too important to the colonists. Jake, bring Gaea here. Do it quietly. I don't want to attract attention at this point."

"She's not going to like it," he warned. "You know Amonite feeling on the subject."

"She'd like it less if we moved without consulting her."

Karmikel was not long in returning with the Councilwoman.

Gaea of Amon had realized from the moment Jake had first approached her that there was a matter of some importance behind this request for her presence in his caravan, and now, looking from one to the other of the off-worlders, she felt a dull throb of fear begin to beat deep within her. Something was decidedly amiss.

She took the seat Islaen offered her. "You wanted to see me?"

The Commando nodded. "A matter's come up that we thought it best to discuss with you privately rather than summoning the full Council at this stage. Your own decision may suffice."

"Go on, Colonel," the older woman told her evenly.

"There's a problem before us, a dirty one. That renegade bull we escaped the other day has been brooding on the encounter, so much so that he's conceived a hatred for everything carrying the human scent and has returned to the plain, or to its edges, rather, in the hope of slaughtering some of us or a few of his own kind at the very least. He'll soon grow bolder and penetrate far enough to meet with potential victims. Since the attempt to drive him off and render him harmless by isolation has failed, the goldbeasts see only one solution. They hate to slay, and because there's so much of the predator in us, they want us to do it for them. Bandit was sent with the request that we do so before some innocent creature, human or grazer, is killed or maimed."

Gaea's eyes flashed furiously. "We did not come to Jade to be turned into a pack of mercenaries, and we shall not begin our history here by slaughtering any population's outcasts!"

"Yet by refusing, you'll be starting that history with the denial of the first serious request, the very first request of any sort, your placesharers have made of you," the guerrilla said quietly.

The Councilwoman controlled her anger with some difficulty. "You were right to bring this question before me, Colonel, though I wish it were one never raised."

"The beast is quite insane and deadly dangerous to every living thing around him," Sogan told her.

She looked at him sharply. The assurance on him seemed to be that of personal knowledge rather than mere belief in the reports of others.

"You are certain of that, Captain? Humans have been used before now, tricked into working great ill."

"I faced that bull. His condition was obvious even before I had the opportunity to compare him with normal specimens of his kind."

Gaea frowned deeply. "If that be true, then his death is both a necessity and a relief for the creature himself."

She sighed. "Amon has a harsh criminal code, and we are a people who prefer to settle matters quickly and decisively, yet I am very loath to order this. I do not want to make very nearly our first official act on Jade one of bloodshed."

"I'll do it," Jake Karmikel said suddenly. "As your liaison officer, I have a responsibility to the colony, but I'm not part of it, and I, too, encountered the beast. I believe this does need to be done."

The Amonite woman was silent for several long minutes.

"Very well, but think on it before you make a final decision. No Jadite animal, whatever the provocation, will be murdered with blasters or lasers or pellet guns, nor will we permit the use of traps or poison. If you do choose to face that bull, it must be as one of Jade's own predators, with only your wits and your body's skills and a knife in place of the claws we humans otherwise lack completely."

She fixed her eyes on Bandit, who cringed visibly beneath her stare.

"Colonel Connor, tell your gurry to inform both grazers and her own kind that renegade goldbeasts are the concern of the herd and shall be handled by the herd as always in the past. We do not intend to interfere in their affairs apart from defending ourselves when absolutely necessary, nor shall we attempt to relieve them of pressure from Jade's predators. Humans have maimed too many worlds and have quite literally destroyed some by disrupting their natural balances. We have no intention of permitting that to happen to Jade of Kuan Yin."

Her manner softened. The chick looked so small and frightened. "I am not really angry with you, Little Bandit. I know you are but the messenger, being the only gurry who can talk to us."

She glanced at Islaen. "Will she be able to comprehend much of that?"

"I think so," she said, barely restraining herself from smiling openly at the chick's deft deflecting of the unpleasant emotion. "I'll go over it with her when she's less excited."

That probably would not even be necessary. Bandit understood human speech even if she could not communicate with others, and her grasp of involved concepts was growing ever stronger.

The Councilwoman's eyes fixed all three of them. "Do not feel compelled to do this. Control of their own kind is the goldbeasts' responsibility. I do not want my people pressured into undertaking it, and I am not putting pressure on you."

"That's understood," Jake said.

"Talk it over among yourselves. I will accept no decision from you until you have done so."

"Jake, don't do it," Islaen pleaded as soon as the three of

them were alone once more. "It's not worth the risk."

He shrugged. "You're making a lot out of it. Some barbarian hunters do the same thing or near enough to it nearly every day."

"We're not hunters! This goes somewhat beyond survival training and living off the land, and you know it."

"If I'm killed, the goldbeasts'll know better than to ask it a second time, won't they?"

He reined his temper. "I don't intend to get hurt, and you don't have to involve yourself, so there's no need for you to get so excited. I haven't asked you to back me."

"You know damn well that I will, Jake Karmikel! There isn't anyone else on this accursed rock with a fraction of even as much skill as we have."

For the first time, the redhead hesitated. "I don't know, Islaen. You heard Gaea."

"Predators often hunt in groups. Besides, if you think I'd let you go and get yourself torn up without having so much as someone around to wield a renewer ray, you're a deal madder than that bull."

"I probably am anyway," he agreed with something of his old humor.

His eyes clouded again. "It is risky, though, and maybe not worth putting both of us on the line."

"Rot! If one can be risked, two can. You have little choice anyway. Bandit knows more or less where the bull is, and I won't let her lead you if you insist upon going alone. You might lose days trying to find him by yourself, and he'd be almost certain to strike before you did, rendering the whole project pointless."

Sogan looked from one to the other of them. "I, for one, oppose this, but if you are determined to go through with it, let us begin now. The morning is no longer young, and we have no way of knowing how long it will be before that creature makes his move. According to Bandit, he is still more or less keeping to the base of the hills where predators are few, but he knows his targets are out here and will eventually risk coming for them."

Karmikel whirled to face him. "Forget it, Sogan! Islaen and I can both handle knives as if we were born with them in our hands, and we grew up dealing with animals at least vaguely similar to goldbeasts. You've had no experience with them at all."

"No," he agreed calmly, "but I can tell you when that specific bull is near, and I can tell you when he is prepared to charge."

"We'll have Bandit," Islaen pointed out quickly.

"Bandit knows generally where he is and maybe can find him precisely, but his madness makes his intentions difficult for her to read save in a broad sense. She might not be able to interpret them quickly enough in an emergency. Beyond all else, she is young and has never witnessed combat. We cannot know how she will react."

He looked apologetically at the chick, but she offered no protest. She realized he was fighting to accompany them and would do nothing to help deny him a place.

"Don't you think I can bring your wife back?" Jake asked sourly.

Sogan's eyes sparkled although his expression did not otherwise change. "Friend, from what I have seen of this lady's performance in a wilderness, she is more likely to bring both of us back than the other way around."

The Noreenan man laughed, and the dark mood vanished from him. "Leave it to an Arcturian to come out with the stark truth and let the ego be damned! —Come if you have a mind for it."

Islaen's eyes fell, but she raised them again in a moment. "I guess you had best do a bit of research into goldbeast anatomy, Jake."

"Aye, Colonel. I'm on my way—"

"Not yet," she said quickly. "I mentioned renewers. Have the Amonites received theirs yet?"

"You're joking! After the way they saved your Admiral's legs? Several of the new hand-sized ones were on their first equipment requisition. They even have a regrowth, but that's a might bulky for this jaunt."

"Hopefully, we won't need either, but collect a ray anyway. Be sure it's functioning."

"Aye, Colonel."

He gave her a smart salute and dashed from the caravan.

Sogan started to follow at a more sedate pace to prepare their flier, but the woman stopped him.

"Varn, wait. I must talk to you."

He frowned slightly, knowing she was opposed to his going. It was a poor sign that she was using speech and holding her mind sealed.

"Aye?"

"Can you influence that bull at all?"

The man shook his head. "No. His madness intervenes. I tried when we clashed before."

She sighed. "Too bad. I'd hoped that might give us some kind of an out."

"Would you have me lull the beast while you slew him?"

"No! You might have convinced him to withdraw!"

"Your pardon, Colonel. I misread you there."

"It was badly put."

Suddenly, her eyes lifted to lock with his. "Varn, if you do come, your role, apart from giving information and maybe warning, must be that of a spectator, unless we're forced to back off altogether."

She forestalled his protest. "No, hear me out. Gaea was definite about the means we must use to accomplish this deed, and your knife work simply isn't good enough, not nearly good enough. If you tried to close with that bull, you'd only get one or both of us mauled trying to protect you."

"I am to watch you be torn and make no move to aid you?" he demanded stiffly.

"If need be. —Varn, we're trying to avoid setting a dark precedent here. I don't think we should involve ourselves at all, no human should, but Jake has elected to take it on. I don't know why he did, but I can't just let him go at it alone, or, worse, with one of these Amonites. There'd be a tragedy then for a fact."

"There could still be a tragedy."

"Aye, though Jake and I are both able."

"You do not wish me to accompany you?" he asked bluntly.

"No, I don't. I know you too well. You won't find it easy standing by, especially if there's real trouble, and I'd rather spare you that."

"Do you imagine waiting here would be easier, with my imagination for company and depending upon a possibly terrified little gurry for news?"

He shook his head. "No, Islaen Connor. If it must be mine only to watch and wait, then at least let it be where I can see what is happening as it occurs. If it becomes necessary to break it off, I could then pull you out."

She sighed. "Very well, Admiral. I yield. I knew you'd say that, or I should have joined Jake's protest."

Her voice hardened. "I must have your word that you'll comply with my terms. I can't allow this hunt to take place only to have it fail in its primary purpose."

The man stiffened, but he gave her no argument. She would not bend in this, and he knew he would have demanded the same assurance of her were their positions reversed.

"As you will," he replied, spitting out the words as if they choked him. "I shall not put you in jeopardy by attempting what my skills cannot carry, and I shall abide by the Councilwoman's command in letter and spirit and refrain from using the weapons with which I am well conversant."

He turned on his heel, not waiting for her to speak again. "I shall be with the flier. When you are ready, join me there."

TEN

THE COMMANDO VEHICLE streaked across the plain but slowed once it neared the hills.

"I wonder how long it'll be before we spot him?" Jake Karmikel said as much to himself as to his companions. "He should be around here somewhere according to what your gurry told you."

"He may have retreated a few miles into the high country," Islaen suggested. "Bandit says predators tried to jump him last night. That would've given him a scare."

"But he's mad, driven to slay—"

"His interest is in the bringing of death, not in suffering it himself," Sogan interjected. "Islaen may be right. According to Bandit, such renegades normally starve themselves into impotence in short order, but this one has continued to maintain his strength. His survival instinct is still functioning, at least partially."

Jake's lips tightened a little. They would not be able to spot the creature nearly as readily in the more broken country of the hills, scarcely before he himself saw them. That would give them precious little time to prepare themselves to receive his attack.

"Take her down as far as you can and go in slow."

The Arcturian nodded. "I intend that, but let us sweep this

outer region first. He may have gone back only a little space and have ventured out again or perhaps not have retreated at all. In any event, we shall quickly discover if he is here or not."

"It'll be a break for us if he is."

"We shall find him. Both Bandit and I will be seeking with mind as well as eyes."

"You think you can pick him up at any real distance?" Karmikel asked curiously.

Sogan shrugged. "At some distance, but how far I cannot say. That depends upon how powerfully he is transmitting and whether the emotions involved are strong or mild. His touch is very distinctive, however," he added, concealing the revulsion he felt at the memory of it. "Any contact at all will be sufficient for me to identify it."

The woman took no part in their discussion. She had grown very quiet in the last quarter hour as her awareness centered upon the gurry, and she was now watching Bandit with a concern which was rapidly transforming into fear.

The chick had not claimed her normal place on Islaen's shoulder but rather was huddled in her lap. She made no effort to speak, and her feathers were ruffled, not stiffly as in anger or agitation, but fluffed out in the manner of a seriously ailing bird.

"What is it, Love?" she asked gently.

Nothing. The reply was curt and sharp, very unlike the gurry's customary manner of answering.

Now Sogan, too, looked at her in concern. The same thought that filled his consort's mind was in his as well, that they had been wrong about the suitability of human food for the little Jadite creature, that they had poisoned her with it.

His mind joined with Bandit's.

He relaxed after a moment. "She is well," he told the others. "She is merely upset. Gurries do not witness the slaying of renegades. They are deeply fond of goldbeasts and do not like to have them brought down, whatever the reason. She did not wish to trouble us by letting us know how much all this upsets her until I convinced her that our worry for her was far more painful for us."

Jake had been leaning forward, nearly as concerned as the other two. Now his eyes flared as he fixed them on his former Commander.

"What kind of savages are you to drag her out here?" he exploded. "We can manage well enough with eyesight and the Admiral's powers without brutalizing gurries!"

"We didn't know, Jake," she said patiently, but her attention remained on the chick. "He's right, though. We can go on from here ourselves. We never wanted to hurt you so."

Bandit will help! You are unhappy, and you will do it.

"No one's forcing us. —Return to camp now. We really can't let you come farther."

Nooo!

Islaen gave a cry of pain as the gurry's sharp claws pierced the material of her trousers and closed on the flesh beneath.

She hastily withdrew her hands. "All right! You win! Just let me go, will you? It's one thing to be bloodied by a goldbeast, but I'll never live it down if I come back battered by a gurry."

She glared at her other companions. "Stop laughing, you two! That happened to hurt."

"Doubtless," Sogan agreed when he could manage to obey her, "but it was very therapeutic for our feisty little comrade. She is in fine form now."

That was true enough, and Islaen stroked her with her forefinger.

"Well, stop looking like you've just whipped a wolf pack with a derelict and get to work. You said you wanted to help."

The Commando officer settled back in her seat. She was well pleased that the incident had occurred. It had dispelled the gloom, the aura of doom, which had been oppressing their spirits. They would work and fight better because of it.

She frowned slightly to herself. Why had it clung so to them in the first place? Surely, this task was no joy and no sinecure, but neither was it in any sense impossible or even monstrously difficult. By the Spirit ruling space, she and Jake had fought men, brave, dedicated, superbly trained and equipped humans. This was, after all, only a beast, however dangerous.

Aye, Colonel, but goldbeasts have shown themselves to be something more than that, the Arcturian's mind responded suddenly, *and this one is mad. That in itself is frightening since it adds enormously to the unknown factors in a duel with him. You would have reason in plenty for uncertainty even were you fully convinced of the necessity of this course.*

You're not either, are you?

I told you I was not. It is worthy enough but not sufficiently so to warrant the risk. It is goldbeast business, not human, and it is they who should settle it.

She could feel a glimmer of amusement run through him, as if he were laughing at himself.

There is no point to all this discussing, you know. As a space hound would put it, we have accepted a charter, and now it is ours to carry it. The time for pondering is over.

He fell silent after that and remained quiet in mind and tongue as they completed the search of the flatlands and penetrated deeper and still deeper into the hills.

Suddenly, the woman heard him draw a sharp breath. "You've picked up something?" she asked eagerly, aloud for Karmikel's sake.

"I think so. Aye. He is down there!"

"Where?" demanded the second man.

"About four miles farther in, I believe. We cannot see him yet."

"The readings? What are they like?" Islaen pressed.

Sogan did not respond for several seconds as he strove to understand the information he was receiving.

"He radiates anger chiefly. It has no specific focus, and anything moving near him would be likely to trigger an active manifestation of it. The blood lust does not burn quite as strongly as I recall. He apparently slew the predators who attacked him last night and is still more or less satiated so that he is content to feed quietly for the moment."

He shook his head. "I am sorry. These readings are very disjointed, and even with Bandit's full help, I cannot be certain my interpretations are entirely accurate. He does not really think at all—"

"You're getting spoiled," the woman observed. "You can't read anything like this clearly elsewhere."

"No, Islaen, but I do not know precisely with what we are dealing. He might be more than a beast or much less depending upon what his madness has done to his other faculties, and of that, I can find no sign."

His hand swept out impatiently. "I am basically back to decoding emotion, and doing right poorly at that since he is not sending logically, not as a sane mind would. Without Bandit's help, I would not be able to interpret half of it, and even now, I cannot so much as determine if last night's attack on him has made him wary, although I believe that may be the case. It would make a difference to your fight if it has."

"It's our business to watch out for that and to allow for his madness in our dealings with him," Jake told him quietly. "You've done very well in forearming us, Admiral."

"What next? The strategy must be yours."

The former guerrilla sighed. "I'd as soon face him right here. There's enough cover around that we might have a chance to bolt for a few seconds if things got too hot, and the ground looks good enough that we wouldn't have to be watching our feet every minute as well as our foe, but I suppose we'll just have to tackle him where we find him unless conditions are altogether impossible there."

Sogan thought for a few seconds. He recalled from their journey through these hills en route to the settlement that there were not many places with so much unbroken, relatively level ground.

"He is not terribly far from us. I could probably fly in low, anger him, and draw him back to you . . ."

Bandit will go.

"No!"

No danger, the chick said calmly. *Gurries always scout renegades, and they always chase us. They get angry, but they don't really want to hurt. This one's mean, but even he's content to scare us. Besides,* she added reasonably, *I can fly. He can't.*

"Go on, Love," Islaen told her, "but don't take any chances. There's no need for that."

"Stay linked with us," Sogan ordered as she took wing. "We'll need all the information we can get."

Bandit will. Don't worry.

ELEVEN

ONCE THE GURRY was gone from sight, the Arcturian brought his vehicle down. "You should not have long to wait," he told the Noreenans as they left it, then he took to the air again without further comment.

Islaen's heart felt heavy. She knew how much he hated this part of it, having to remain airborne during the confrontation, useless unless they or the situation called for a rescue, a call which would terminate the mission. She would detest that role as passionately had their positions been reversed, would suffer the same lash of unmerited shame and self-loathing.

She put that from her mind then and studied their proposed battleground carefully.

The footing was not so good as it had seemed from the air, she saw now. The thick vegetation was not grass or ferns but a kind of vine that could trip one if luck went against him, and a considerable amount of loose rock was concealed under it. It was not terribly bad, however, and there appeared to be no holes or sudden drops. They could have done much worse.

"No trees," Jake moaned as he joined her after completing his own tour of the place.

She smiled. "We'd be a little hard pressed to find one on Jade."

The woman was sorry for that lacking as well. They were a

prime safety feature on Noreen, where every pasture had several, and she and her brothers had spent many an hour in their branches over the years awaiting rescue from the attentions of testy angoras.

They remained standing together, discussing possible strategy, until Sogan's thought warned that the goldbeast was nearing the place in great anger. He had followed Bandit casually enough, but they were upwind of him, and he had taken their scent a couple of minutes previously. It was one he remembered well, and all his rage at their having escaped him on their first meeting was now upon him in full force.

Once the woman had relayed that information to Jake, and Sogan had answered their few questions, he severed the contact. He would not link with his consort again until the issue was resolved lest he distract or unsettle her. If fortune willed against them, he might never join mind with her again.

Islaen Connor moved away from her companion and drew her combat knife, although she might not be called upon to use it. Karmikel was to meet the animal's charge and carry the fight. She might only back him or might more actively aid him depending upon how the attack developed.

Their strategy was simple in the main. It had to be; they had few options as to what they could do.

Goldbeasts were big, powerfully built creatures, and their lungs and hearts were buried deeply beneath heavy muscle and bone, equally safe from predators' claws and the knives in the humans' hands. The abdominal organs could be cut, aye, but death would not come immediately, very likely not nearly quickly enough to prevent his taking vengeance on his slayers. The bone of the skull and face was solid and too thick for a knife powered by no more than their muscles to penetrate.

They had but two possible targets, the eyes or the blood vessels of the neck and throat. Of these, the former were small and narrow, making a difficult entryway for a knife in practice, although a kill through the eyes was theoretically possible. It was for the last that they must go, for the neck, despite the fact that they would have to come in very close to the deadly, flailing hooves and dare the crushing speed of the creature in order to make a strike there.

A blaster fired at very close range would make the kill considerably easier. . . .

The Commando-Colonel angrily banished that thought. Federation weapons would aid their fight and all but insure its success, aye, but they were here as symbols, not as mere hunters. Gaea of Amon was right. Her people had come to Jade to join with the planet, not to overpower or enslave. Interference in this affair was bad enough, but to introduce off-world murder tools would be to once again sink into humanity's ancient, evil response to opposition, the merciless slaughter, even to the point of genocide, of offending species or peoples. That precedent must never be given the opportunity to root on this untainted world, whatever the cost to two Noreenans who chose to involve themselves in something that was, in truth, no business at all of theirs.

They need not fight at all, of course. The option to flee was always open to them. Both she and Karmikel chose to ignore that course for the moment, but neither of them rejected it outright. This task they had accepted was not of such importance that they were required to die trying to complete it if it could not reasonably be done. If their efforts proved useless, they were fully prepared to break and run, preferably into the wilder land around or by airlift if that proved impossible, although that latter move would mark the end and failure of their mission. Sogan had ropes at ready to which they could cling should a quick escape be necessary.

Tension played painfully along Jake Karmikel's nerves as he faced the direction from which Sogan said the bull would come. He grasped his knife tightly but could find no comfort in its familiar hilt. It seemed such a tiny thing to set against so great a monster . . . .

When would the goldbeast come? This waiting was an agony!

A bugling roar ripped into him, like that which the renegade had given at their first encounter but carrying a far heavier element of fury.

Stark fury. The raw, primal force of it paralyzed every muscle of his body, so that he stood frozen, helplessly waiting.

The huge beast tore into view, outpacing even the gurry in his rage.

The bull saw his quarry and bellowed again but instantly braked his run, continuing only the few steps necessary to maintain his balance. He remained where he stopped, quiet now, glaring balefully at the man out of his pale, strange eyes.

Karmikel's heart beat fast and hard. His muscles were free again, but he kept still, waiting to see what the goldbeast would do.

He liked this halt far less than he would have the wild charge he had been anticipating. It was proof that though his opponent might be mad, he was anything but mindless. He had not slain those predators last night and maybe others before them entirely through luck and blind force but through at least some exercise of skill and reason. The experience had also apparenly left him cautious about recklessly challenging one foe while another was near, ready to strike at side or back. The Arcturian had been right about that.

Still, Jake waited. Some move must come soon, and that would release him. Until then, he dared do nothing, either attack or flee. He was too far from cover and the goldbeast was too near for him to try anything until the bull first made a choice for him to counter.

The goldbeast's wild bugle and his charge came in the same moment, but Karmikel was ready for it. He leaped aside, away from the hurtling body, barely avoiding the sudden, vicious side thrust of the foreleg.

Jake had not expected that last, and the additional, last-moment effort required to escape it put him enough off balance that he was unable to make any offensive move himself, although he did keep both his feet and full control of himself.

He was ready for the next charge. When the bull came for him, he deftly spun away, returning swiftly enough to slash his knife through the black's side.

The bull's speed and sharpness of movement were astonishing for so huge a creature, and although the man was able to keep away from him and succeeded in bloodying him several times, he could not get in a fatal or otherwise telling blow. Gradually he could feel weariness begin to bite in earnest upon him. . . .

Islaen Connor watched the fight for several minutes, her expression growing ever tighter, ever grimmer.

It was apparent what Karmikel was trying to do and equally apparent that he would not accomplish it. He could not. The goldbeast was agile and strong, and he had learned well how to deal with predators alone during his exile from the herd. He need only wait, wear Jake down, and finish him off when he faltered at last in his exhaustion.

They were tactics not to be faulted. The renegade would gain the day, and gain it soon. No man could keep going long as her comrade was doing.

The former guerrilla was almost fast enough. If the bull could be distracted for a few seconds, giving Jake an opening . . .

She sprang toward them, but the black had kept watch on her all this while, and she found her way blocked even as was Karmikel's by the wickedly sharp hooves.

She could not get near the vital throat area, but that was not essential to her purpose. The Commando moved for another target, not the side but the flank.

Islaen could not reach even that. A rush of despair swept through her. Was she to fail Jake utterly?

She started to make a quick feint to draw the beast's attention to her, but suddenly, her foot struck a loose stone, and she nearly went down.

A moment was all she required to steady herself, but the goldbeast saw her totter and came for her with the speed of a projectile, determined to finish off this one of his foes quickly. Islaen raised her knife in an instinctive, futile effort to ward him off, but she knew even as she prepared her defense that her doom was on her.

A keening shriek sounded over the battlefield as a tiny brown missile hurtled from out of the sky, directly at the charging bull's face.

Bandit's assault was unexpected, utterly without precedent in Jade's history, and it was nigh unto irresistible in the sheer fury of it despite her laughably inconsequential size. She dove for the right eye, that farthest from the guerrilla, and struck it, tearing madly with her sharp, supple claws.

The woman did not waste her chance. She recovered herself and leaped for her temporarily heedless target as he bellowed his agony and tossed his head and body violently to rid himself of his minute tormentor.

The beast's own movement aided her blow, and rather than slicing along his flesh as she had intended, the knife plunged straight into it, burying itself to its very hilt.

This, the goldbeast could not ignore. He roared and leaped, tearing the weapon from her hands. In the same instant, he struck out with his hind legs.

Islaen whirled as soon as her knife was wrenched from her, but her opponent moved far too quickly. Both hooves caught her squarely in the side even as she turned, lifting her and driving her several feet back before she crashed to lie motionless upon the battered ground.

Jake did not wait to watch the result of the gurry's attack. He knew he had been given his chance and knew that he was not likely to be granted a second. He would have but a moment in which to act, and as soon as the black's attention shifted from him, he sprang for the broad back.

His legs automatically tightened against the sweat-soaked hair, and even while the goldbeast made his dire leap, the Noreenan drove his blade into his neck.

Again and once again, first to the left and then the right, he struck as blood shot skyward from the punctured arteries.

He clung desperately to his place, praising all Noreen's beneficent gods for the hours he and his mates had spent trying to see who could remain longest on the back of a wildly bucking young angora bull or steer.

What had been sport then was giving him his life now. The black was doomed, but to be thrown off before the animal's last strength failed him was to die along with him. Nothing falling beneath those pounding hooves could survive them.

After what seemed an eternity but was actually only seconds, the bull stumbled, staggered, and went down.

Jake jumped clear when he felt the goldbeast begin to topple. He landed squarely on his feet, ready to run should the impossible have occurred and the bull be only shamming his collapse, but caution was now needless. The great creature was dead and had been dead even as he had fallen.

He stared at the monstrous, blood-stained body, scarcely able in that instant to realize that the victory was truly his.

Consciousness of it came to him in the next second and excitement with it, and he turned to seek his comrade. It was then that he saw Islaen.

TWELVE

SOGAN WAS ALREADY with the felled Commando, kneeling beside her, cradling her head on his knees while he systematically played the clumsy-looking renewer over her body. The blood-stained gurry was perched close by them, squeaking pitiously.

The Noreenan thought for a moment that his own heart would cease to beat.

Not now. Not after all the danger they had faced, the hardships they had endured. Not for so little.

He began walking slowly toward them. He could not bring himself to run, to hasten the confirmation of his fear.

Sogan's face was a mask, but he was starkly white, as if his eyes looked, not into simple death, but into the core of his world's direst hell while the one support holding him out of it slowly crumbled away.

He was using the renewer, not merely holding it, but that could be no more than a futile gesture born of shock and despair.

Jake groaned in his mind. He was responsible for this. He had done it with his stubborn insistence . . .

He had almost reached his comrades by then. The Arcturian either saw him, or, more likely, Bandit informed him of his approach, and he looked up.

"She is all right. Consciousness has not yet returned, but I believe the renewer has taken care of the damage."

His voice tightened slightly. "There had been considerable shattering of bone."

Karmikel scarcely heard him, so deep was his relief. His own eyes confirmed the former Admiral's words, for although Islaen was pale beyond her wont, a delicate, living flush played beneath her pallor.

Even as he watched, she gave a deep sigh, and her eyelids fluttered open.

She smiled up at Varn. "I'm not hurt," she assured him. "How's Jake? And my valiant little Bandit?"

"Both fine," the Noreenan said quickly. "I have a few bruises and scrapes, which I amply merit, but that's about it."

"Praise the Spirit of Space for that!"

The woman started to sit up, but her consort would not permit her to take her own weight and gently raised her.

"Easy," he warned. "You are to rest until Dr. Kurmut can examine you properly. I am no medical expert to trust completely in my use of that ray."

"It doesn't require much talent," she remarked dryly, but she let him have his way; in truth, she was tired and still very sore, and she welcomed the support of his arm.

Her eyes widened as they fell on Bandit. The chick was literally soaked with drying blood. "Jake, you said she was all right!"

"She is, Colonel," Sogan told her. "None of that is hers. There was too much risk of being smashed by the bull's hooves or against his head to chance letting go, and so she held on until he went down, same as your friend here. —Jake is also pretty well covered, but the effect is not quite as dramatic on him."

"Naturally not," Karmikel responded, compelling himself to speak lightly. "I'm only a human, not a cute little gurry."

He bent to stroke the Jadite mammal and then brought his attention back to the woman, who did not look at all convinced despite their assurances and Bandit's own.

"Look, Islaen, be reasonable. If she were hurt, you'd still be lying there on the ground while we fussed over her. Sometimes, I think she exercises a quiet, efficient form of magic, the way she manages to get people to tend to her wants."

"She does indeed, friend." Islaen studied the normally immaculate hen critically. "One of you, get me a canteen and some washing creme. It's time we got that mess off her."

Bandit drew herself to her full height. *Even very young chicks know how to wash,* she told them primly. *Besides, this is better for now. It will help Bandit.*

She took wing but hovered over them a moment. *Go back. I'll find flier.*

With that, she flew off in the direction of the plain, leaving the two who understood her looking after her with bemused surprise.

The Commando translated what she had said for Jake's benefit and straightened herself. She was relieved to find movement not quite so painful a procedure this time.

"Shall we be going, Comrades?"

Once again, Sogan would not allow her to rise. He quickly swept her up into his arms. "You ride in the back this time, Colonel," he informed her.

"Stay with her," Jake suggested. "I'll take the controls."

Sogan nodded his thanks and gently settled the woman in her place. Islaen did not protest although she thought they were both carrying their concern to the ridiculous. She lacked the energy to begin a useless argument right now, and this was not one she had a hope of winning.

"Are you about set back there?" Karmikel asked.

"Aye."

The woman forgot her weariness. The Arcturian's shields had slipped a little when he had replied to Jake's question, enough to let her glimpse something of what lay behind them even now, with the incident over and the danger past.

It's finished, Varn, her mind said very softly. *Let it go.*

He made her no answer at first, but seeing that he had betrayed himself, he opened himself completely to her.

Had I lost you, I should have lost everything. My life would have been utterly emptied once more, and this time, there would have been no cause powerful enough to justify a fraction of such sacrifice.

His eyes closed. *Islaen, swear to me that this will not happen again, that you will not risk yourself a second time like this without true need to drive you, or ever again exclude me from full participation in your work. That was part of the vow we made to one another, and I never want to have to bear any further violation of it.*

She pressed closely against him, letting her own love and her grief for all he had endured run into him.

Not for all I love or revere would I have had you tortured like this. That's why I wanted you away from it. —No, it won't happen again, not if I have the power to choose otherwise.

She looked up at him, caught and held his gaze. *I can't promise more, Varn. I mightn't be able to keep my word.*

That is sufficient, my Islaen. Fate and the gods have their plans for us, and many of their workings cannot be foreseen.

They fell truly silent then, maintaining contact but not actually speaking until the gurry demanded their more active attention, first mentally from a distance and then with voice as she claimed her customary place a few minutes later. She was clean again, though her feathers were still dark and damp after her bath, and there was an air of satisfaction about her.

Islaen is well now? she demanded, looking at each of the humans in turn, as if daring them to lie to her.

"I am indeed, and it's in a large part thanks to you. —What of your own mission just now? Did you complete it?"

Bandit did. Bandit told the goldbeasts and gurries all about it. I said how afraid I was and how you were hurt, and I let them see how close I came to it all. They know humans aren't predators now and are sorry for pushing this onto you and almost causing you to die. They would've done it easier, with less effort and grief, even to he who's now gone. They won't suggest anything like it again.

Bandit seemed spent after so long and sustained a communication, but she nigh unto glowed under the admiration her companions poured out upon her.

"You're truly a wonder," the woman told her happily, "and you're wise. Going to the herd so quickly and in that state of appearance was a really brilliant move. Many a human wouldn't have acted half so effectively."

"No, we wouldn't."

She looked swiftly upon the Noreenan man. He had been silent and withdrawn during most of the return journey thus far. Some of it was out of consideration for them, for Varn's readily understood need to have her to himself for a while, but a great weight lay upon his spirit, all but crushing him.

"Jake, if you don't stop radiating gloom at this level,

you're going to drive me right into a massive depression."

"It's not funny," he retorted sharply. "I almost got you killed. I don't know why I insisted on taking on this hunt, what I was trying to prove. . . ."

"You wouldn't be Jake Karmikel if you weren't impulsive. Commando service might have checked its broadest manifestations, but slay it, no. Besides, in this case, your instincts were quite right. We've ended the threat posed by that renegade and, thanks to Bandit's help, so managed it as to leave the goldbeasts with enough of a guilt load that they won't ask the Amonites for a similar service again. —My friend, you've pulled off a major diplomatic coup with this little jaunt."

The woman fell silent suddenly and withdrew into herself.

"What is it, Islean?" her consort asked, sensing trouble on her.

"I don't know," she answered after a moment. "A thought trying to be born. It seemed to rise up for an instant, but it's gone again."

"Let it be, then. If it is important, it will come back to you but, Commando-Colonel Connor, I would not have you try yourself even so far as to seek for it. I was in deadly earnest when I said you were to rest this day."

"Varn! Oh, very well."

Her tone became firm. "Just don't let me hear any more recriminations from either of you, or I'll be forced to turn myself into a psychomedic. If all Jade's problems can be solved as easily as this one was, she'll be a paradise indeed. Let it lie there."

Sogan smiled faintly. "As you will, Colonel."

Bandit fluttered from the woman's shoulder to the back of the driver's seat. *Go higher! The herd is waiting.*

Islaen relayed the order. "Do what she wants, Jake. She's rather the heroine of the day, after all."

"Doesn't everyone always do what she wants?" he grumbled good-naturedly. He obeyed promptly, however, increasing the flier's speed as he did so, and soon the great river plain was before and below them.

The Commando frowned. Something was amiss.

She gasped as the answer came to her. The herd was clearly visible, but not as she had seen it before. Every one of the mighty animals comprising it was standing on alert, every one facing the hill country. The gurry had meant precisely that when she had said they were waiting. They were watching for a sight of the homecoming flier.

For one instant, the same nagging thought embryo which had teased her earlier quickened again, but then it faded entirely. They had been seen, and a bugling call arose from the world below. It reverberated wildly over the plain, the salute and welcome of three-quarters of a billion creatures for those who had served them so well and very nearly at such terrible cost in a fight they should never have been asked to undertake.

THIRTEEN

ISLAEN CONNOR CAREFULLY slid out from beneath her blankets and drew on her clothes as quickly as she could. However comfortable these caravans might be in most ways, their limited heating systems left much to be desired for one born on Noreen's mild plains, at least until Kuan Yin had been up for a while and had driven out the chill with her warm rays.

She had been certain Bandit would stay with Varn, but the gurry fluttered up to the open shelf above the bed, her feathers ruffled against the cold, obviously intending to accompany the woman.

Islaen carefully resettled the covers around her husband, then sighed to herself as she straightened again. Even in sleep, his face was tense, guarded, a look he rarely lost save when they were alone in the depths of space, and not often even there.

So much fear and pain, she thought, and such a great portion of it was solidly founded in stark reality.

We have our work before us, Little One, her mind whispered to the gurry chick, then she quietly stole from the cubicle and from the caravan itself lest she should wake him.

The Commando moved away from the camp, walking quickly although the countless stars and Jade's baker's dozen of moons still gleamed brightly in the ebony sky above her.

She had no fear of traveling amidst the goldbeasts now and none at all of meeting with predators, not with the gurries to warn if any dared approach the herd.

Only when she neared the great river did her pace become more cautious. Fewer animals were bedded here, and she knew that amphibian hunters did haunt the bank, although not normally so close to the grazers.

She walked a little way along the edge of the bank until she found a large stone. It was flat and clean, and she seated herself upon it.

All the world was very silent, and she felt quite alone in it, alone save for Bandit, now riding shielded from the sharp breeze within her service jacket. The encampment was but a dot behind her to her left, the nearest pods only dark lumps in the general grayness.

To her right, before her, was the still-invisible river, its waters rushing by with a constant lapping hiss.

Dawn came while she waited there, and the light strengthened rapidly until the stream was clearly visible beneath the steep bank on whose lip she sat.

The sight of it fascinated and soothed her, as running water always did. The volume of it was awe-inspiring. Individual bodies bearing the name of seas on some of the more arid worlds were not so broad, and this had a depth worthy of its breadth. The current was strong enough that its sweep was clearly perceptible.

There must have been a heavy storm farther north, she thought, although the weather had been grand here. The river looked to be somewhat roiled, and there was quite a bit of debris flowing with it, chiefly branches and brush, even what looked to be entire bushes. Either fierce wind or rain had broken them off, or else the volume of water had risen past its usual line and was tearing growing things away from its upper banks. The yellow color was deeper, too, indicating an increase in the ever-present load of sediment.

The woman opened her jacket so that Bandit might poke her head out. "Keep watch for us now, Love," she cautioned. "You'll know if any amphibians come around long before I will."

Her finger automatically began to caress the little head. She felt better now. Something had been bothering her, nagging at her since last evening, and she had come out here to be at peace to think for a while, but whatever it was had gone again, vanished in the stillness and balance all around her.

She reached into her pocket and took out the packet of standard rations she had caught up almost without thinking on her way out of the caravan.

An excited whistling greeted that action, and she looked at the chick in mock dismay before breaking off a few crumbs for her.

"Go easy on this stuff! I know you appear to tolerate our grub well, but I don't want my six-ounce darling turning into a six-ton monster."

Nooo. Gurries are careful!

The woman gave the indignant chick a bit more. "That's good to hear, but I'll say this for you, you're about the only creature I've ever met that actually likes Federation rations."

Good food. A little fills and no work to get it.

Islaen smiled, then grimaced, recalling living for weeks on the tasteless concentrates. "Sometimes the work is worth the results. I'll take real food any day, and so will those of my kind who have come here to live once they get set up and start producing their own."

Jade would supply that in plenty and in variety. She was a planet rich in grains and leaves, roots and fruit, in plants of the water as well as of the land. The Amonites had found a paradise, albeit one in which they must labor to win their livelihood.

That was what they wanted. They wished to be part of their world, giving as well as receiving, prospering but ever earning that prosperity, and Jade of Kuan Yin seemed created to fill their need and purpose.

She was truly a wonderful planet, as marvelous in her complexity as in her bounty, the Commando thought, looking down at the fast-flowing water. This one region was a study in balance and interaction. The great river might not be pretty to one accustomed to bright, clear streams, but it contributed to, indeed was in a large part responsible for, the lushness of the lands it drained.

Yellow water. Yellow banks. Rich, yellow soil to support the luxuriant growth of the plain. . . .

Islaen Connor sat straight. Her hands dropped to her sides as the color left her face and her enormous eyes blazed like discharging blasters.

Varn, get Jake! I want to see you both now, and in private.

Sogan came to his feet almost before he was fully awake. He hurried into his clothes, grabbing his jacket and racing from the caravan within seconds after the summons had reached him.

He ran to the wagon used by the former Commando and slammed his hand against its front, as near as he could reach to the sleeping area. A seeming eternity later, Jake Karmikel came to the door. He had a blanket across his shoulders and was scowling darkly.

"What in space do you think—"

One look at the Arcturian silenced his outburst. "What's up, Sogan?"

"A mind call from Islaen. She is waiting by the river and wants both of us there now, without letting the rest know we have gone."

"No explanation?"

"None," he replied tightly, "but there is fury on her, that and some degree of fear."

FOURTEEN

THE TWO MEN left the camp as quickly as they could without drawing attention to themselves. People would be stirring in most of the caravans by now, and a few were already venturing outside. Any undue noise or haste would be noticed.

With her mind link with Sogan to guide them, they were not long in coming to the Commando-Colonel.

She was standing on the crest of the riverbank, her face white and set and as harsh as outraged Justice. For once, Bandit was not perched on her shoulder but was on the ground, her wings extended and ruffled; she greeted them with a rasping hiss.

"The gurry appears agitated," Sogan observed, although his eyes scarcely flickered to the hen before returning to his consort; such anger was rare to Islaen Connor and boded very ill, for themselves and for those who had sparked it.

"She should be. She's just been learning about human predators." The guerrilla nodded to her former associate. "You were right about Settlement Agent Thurston Sandstone, Jake. He's a viler serpent than any of the scum we blew out of the space over Astarte."

"Start from the beginning, Lass," Karmikel said, but his own tone matched hers.

"He's clever, right enough. Just sit back, let nature take its course, and the river tears would be his for the taking.

"Amon is an arid planet, and her offspring would've settled in here, tended their goldbeasts and farmed their land, and not one of them would have guessed that they were all roosting on top of an activated planetbuster."

Hatred poured from her until Sogan's mind reeled under it, but he made no protest. By all the Federation's many gods, what danger, what treachery, did she see that was driving her so?

Islaen did not even notice his discomfort in the rage that was on her.

"It might take a year. It might take three, but eventually, there would be unusually heavy winter rains throughout the north. Feeder streams would swell, and the river would swell until it poured over its banks or through them or sent one mighty crest sweeping down along all its length. There's not so much as a ten-foot-high bump anywhere on this whole plain to serve as a refuge, and there wouldn't be a single colonist left after it to describe the flood's coming."

Jake snarled a furious oath in Noreen's ancient tongue. Of course! The plot was so clear when she named it. The soil of the plain was formed and fed by river sediment. If the overflows did not come on a yearly basis, they were a frequent enough occurrence that the vast goldbeast herd moved off, farther south to higher, rougher ground, long before winter nipped the lush sweetness of the grass, to avoid the threat of them.

Varn Tarl Sogan had taken on the cold, hard look both his companions had seen on him so often during their years on Thorne when he had stood as chief of the invading fleet they had been sent to combat. He did not share their inner certainty of the inevitability of doom from the river. Space and machines and the life of Navy encampments and of palaces were part of him, but he had little instinctive feeling for the ways of wild worlds despite all his efforts over these last months to acquire that sensitivity to them.

The former Admiral's own people were responsible for this lacking which he himself had not even recognized before his fateful meeting with the Commando unit on Visnu. The Empire's citizens had divorced themselves from any connection with natural phenomena on their own planets centuries before, believing anything of import had either been slaughtered or conquered by their all-powerful machines.

That was a bit of arrant pride, arrant stupidity, he thought bitterly. His kind had not even realized that their supposedly tamed worlds had never been other than tame, seismically dead, geophysically comatose balls of rock blessed with stable, basically acceptable climates challenging only to stark savages. Scant wonder they had been able to secure their survival on their home planets at so early a stage in their history, and turn their energies to the conquest of space and their fellow humans!

Their soldiers had suffered heavily, and, to his mind, often needlessly, because of that complacency and the lack of study and preparation it bred. The Emperor's Navy was superb, the courage and skill of his fighting men of unquestioned excellence, and, especially in the early years of the great conflict, the Arcturian war fleets had swept through the outer Federation Sectors like the undamable fury of the gods.

Occupying the planets thus seized had all too often proved another matter. Time after time, with dismaying regularity, invasion fleets had come down on the unpopulated or sparsely populated barbarian worlds where the surplanetary portion of the War had been fought only to meet with disaster when some native, entirely unexpected violence of the planet herself rose up to annihilate them. That should never have been. The possibility of such perils should have been considered, studied, and measures taken to counter them or lessen their effects if they did strike.

Sogan forced his mind back from the past he could not alter to the present situation. His people had proven helpless when the lands they claimed suddenly opened beneath them or spat fire or the seas rose up in vast, all-crushing walls or winds blew that shattered starships able to withstand both the perils of space and the Federation's mighty death weapons, but their record against the supposedly helpless peoples of the planets they had overwhelmed was, as a whole, no matter for pride either. Most local populations had, often with the help of the legendary Commandos, formed themselves into Resistance forces which usually met with considerable success, sometimes to the point of fighting their invaders into positions of relative impotence, although the cost of their courage had nearly always been high. Sometimes, it had been awesome.

His face hardened. Not all commanders viewed the Empire's honor as he had or could find it in themselves to respect menial-born foes. The brutality with which some of them responded to surplanetary opposition, even to the destruction of entire worlds, had earned for the Emperor's troops a reputation for savagery which still threatened him today, but the mentality and nature necessary for such conduct was hardly limited to the Arcturian race. If Islaen were right now, then Thurston Sandstone of Terra possessed and exercised both in full measure.

His head snapped toward the woman. "A creature who risked laying this trap is not likely to bow down and withdraw at its thwarting."

"No, that he most assuredly won't do. We can count on that if on nothing else."

Jake Karmikel's heart slammed once, painfully, in his breast. The Amonites were like a painted target in their well-known campsite on this shelterless plain. A quick pirate raid could wipe them out within seconds should the attackers consider that their safest course, them and the spaceport tying them to the stars.

"What do we do?"

"Calm down, first of all," the Colonel told him, her chin lifting as she took up responsibility for the colonists' survival. "Our friends have been here for several weeks and will remain here a good two or three months longer. There'll be less activity around Jade near the end of that time as the supply deliveries ease off. That would be a more logical time to pull a raid."

"Greed and impatience could outweigh logic in Sandstone's mind."

"Aye. We'll assemble the settlers as soon as we get back to the camp. I just wanted to run this past you first."

Her lips tightened. "I suppose I was hoping you'd tell me I was lifting blind and navigating right out of the lanes."

"Not a chance, Colonel," Jake told her grimly. He sighed. "I'm not going to like facing those Amonites with this. They've had their share of treachery and then some."

She nodded. "Fate has used them dramatically, if nothing else. Either they're blessed out of all counting by their gods in the rescues they've had, or else they're accursed beyond all hope. —Let's be off, comrades. I, for one, choose to accept the former premise and work in accordance with it."

Sogan's hand stayed her. "Hold a moment. We are going too fast."

"Too fast!" Karmikel exploded. "Those people have to be warned—"

"Against the danger of floods, aye. Tell them of that and of the need to move quickly if the goldbeasts show signs of decamping abruptly, but say nothing of treachery. The settlers will respond poorly to such news, and the man we suspect may not be guilty."

"Not guilty! He proposed that they settle this plain!"

"Possibly through error or, at worst, negligence born of indifference or poor attention to his survey reports."

The Noreenan man gave him a contemptuous look. "Climb off it, Sogan. You're not that innocent."

"I never was innocent," he responded quietly, "but I can testify to what may happen when there is grave overreaction to guilt."

Islaen shuddered in her heart at the memory of his flayed back. Even now, after he had spent a month under renewer treatment, the sight of it sent a chill through her. Before that, it had been the stuff of nightmare.

Jake had fallen silent as well, but she could see that his opinion had not altered.

She shook her head. "I'm afraid I'm with Jake in this, Varn."

The Arcturian gave her a bleak smile. "So am I, Colonel, but if we forget the other possibility, we just might wind up letting our true quarry escape."

"He's right," the Commando agreed after a moment. "Sandstone's the one who sees all the reports, pulls them all together, and he's the one who's in the best position to edit out information or add it to his own ends, but somebody on the next level or so below him might be able to work that kind of cover-up as well. We want to be dead sure before making our move."

"We must be sure," Varn Tarl Sogan told her grimly. Both looked sharply at him. "You're obviously reading something we aren't, Varn," Islaen said. "What is it that you fear?"

"Precipitating something we don't want." His eyes went to the distant camp. "The way I see it, we are walking between ice and fire. A step too far either way means disaster.

"Right now, Sandstone is still hoping for a flood, and by

the look of that river this morning, even to my eyes, his wish may soon come to pass. Failing in that, he will be searching for some other, similar way to strike down the Amonites. While any chance at all of discovering one remains, he will not call in a raid, not unless he is panicked into it."

"How do you know that?" Jake demanded, both annoyed and fascinated by the former Admiral's seeming assurance.

"Because I believe the man is essentially a coward. He knows his personal risk is very slight with a natural disaster to act as his agent. Even if it fails to work his will completely or the danger is discovered in time to avert it entirely, the worst he could expect to face would be a forced premature retirement. In the unlikely event that someone did think there was more to the disaster than a tragic oversight, investigations take time, more than enough for him to grab a few of the stones and vanish, or merely vanish if that were not possible, into some bolthole he doubtless has already prepared."

"But we're investigating now," the Colonel reminded him.

"Aye, and we will do Jade no service if we do not complete the job. —Sandstone is not alone in this. He cannot be. He needs a ship to get the stones and, whatever his wish to handle this business circumspectly, the crew will have to be of a kind all too willing to act more directly. They will have to have been chartered well in advance and will not be ignorant of the means by which he plans to work the colony's destruction. He would have to give them that much assurance to prevent them from moving prematurely. No one but outright pirates would touch it, and they tend to prefer direct, fast action."

Both of his companions nodded but did not interrupt him.

"Sandstone would never be fool enough to give them the stones' location before he was ready to go for them himself, but if we fail to take his hirelings, and he knows himself to be hopelessly trapped, he could well avenge himself by leaking the information to them and letting them work their will on the colonists. Even if we should foil that, he would still have a sort of revenge. A constant, heavy Navy guard would be required until Jade was well enough established and strong enough to see to her own defense, a matter of three or four generations at the very least. He knows how Amonites would bridle under that."

"A direct strike would net him the jewels without any of this maneuvering," Jake commented. "Why are you so certain that he'll go the much harder route, especially with some unruly companions whose goodwill he requires?"

"Because heavy casualties are inevitable to such an attack, and it is far easier to slay indirectly. He will order a raid if he cannot think of a better method to gain his ends, but if he can get Jade to do his butcher work for him, he will avoid having to nerve himself to give the command—and accepting the risk inherent in that—and he would later be able to excuse himself of guilt much more readily."

"Oh, for . . . Killing's killing, Sogan. He's setting them up. It makes no difference how the Amonites actually die."

"Not so. I could not have brought myself to burn unarmed prisoners. Even on Thorne, I switched my blaster to stun several times before bringing down Resistance fighters, and that was during hot battle.

"In space, it was another matter entirely. My flagship was always a prime target whenever our fleets joined with yours, and the fact that I still live is proof that I won each of those duels. When an enemy's screens began to crumble beneath my pletzars, I ordered our fire intensified, annihilating the damaged ship and anywhere from a thousand to four thousand Federation soldiers along with her."

"You were fighting for your own life and the lives of your crew!"

"Aye, but I was doing the same on Thorne and found the slaying more difficult there. —This Sandstone is not war trained, and he is not a young man able to adopt radically new ways readily. He will want to clasp this lie and make himself believe its reality, even if his mind is sick enough to imagine the river tears are his by right and may be taken no matter what cost to others."

Jake shook his head in protest, but Islaen's raised hand silenced him before he could speak.

"He could be right. There have been all too many mass murderers in the history of the Federation's planets, and a large percentage of them never saw their victims, never even knew their names. The most of them couldn't have carried out their order themselves, not if they had to face those they wanted dead."

"All right," the former Commando said, "for the sake of argument, I'll buy what you're saying and assume Sandstone prefers not to attack if he can kill or rob more subtly. That's the ice you mentioned, Admiral. What about the fire?"

"His hirelings. They won't have any such qualms about killing. They will stay passive as long as they think the original plan has any hope of succeeding, but if they come to believe it has failed or if they begin to fear discovery, they will demand the information they need and perhaps force it out of Sandstone if he remains reluctant to give it. Once they have that, they will strike."

Jake merely nodded. A major natural disaster would be to the attackers' advantage since it would provide them with an excellent cover. Thurston Sandstone would be able to travel anywhere on Jade that he chose in its aftermath and bring anyone he desired with him. No one would question or interfere with him.

A direct attempt on the stones was a more dangerous matter and absolutely necessitated the destruction of at least the port. No pirate crew would consider planeting at all, much less remaining on-world for the length of time needed to rape even one river tear deposit while equipment or personnel capable of tracking them or of summoning the Navy or Patrol remained operational.

There would be no direct reason to go after the main body of the settlers in that event if they were not located too close to one of the target deposits, and there was a faint chance that they might be left alone, but they would be burned down if there was any possibility whatsoever of their discovering what was going on. Even the fact of the theft could not be allowed to become known before the jewels were sold or they would be marked goods. The stones were too rare to conceal their probable origins in that event, and no open market would handle them, and perhaps no fence either, not even at a minute fraction of their value.

From the raiders' point of view, there were a great many advantages to the total annihilation of all human life on Jade if it could be wrought quickly and fairly easily.

Even if the settlers' camp did escape, it would make little difference to the colony itself. The loss of the port and its personnel was too heavy a blow for so young a settlement to survive.

All three were quiet for a time as the same gloomy conclusions filled their minds.

Sogan shook them off first. "One thing I do not understand. Why involve the Amonites in the first place? The robbery would be easier to conceal if they never realized there was a target at all."

"True, but there was apparently too great a chance of spontaneous discovery and some very embarrassing questions," Karmikel suggested, "especially once they had chosen a nomadic life-style. I understand one of the deposits is near this place, as a matter of fact, although I don't know the location, of course."

"The camp should be moved soon, then," Islaen remarked. "If only we had some idea of the time left to us!"

Her shoulders squared. "Jake, contact Horus. I want the survey reports, all of them from the first discovery on, pulled. Get the explorers' personal notes and run them against the official documents at each level of processing. Have them transmitted directly to me on the *Maid*."

"The *Maid*? Where—"

"I have to see Thurston Sandstone. I might be able to pick up something of his intentions, and at the very least, I should be able to determine whether we're dealing with a madman or a monster."

"Insane?" The Noreenan man shook his head. "I know you've been considering it, but I sincerely hope he isn't, Islaen. We couldn't even depend on logic then. That would be an unpleasant complication."

"Most unpleasant but also very likely, I fear. As for logic, that often goes to the winds in a major crime anyway."

"Most killers have their reason firmly in place," he reminded her, "though I'll grant you this thing seems so vile as to say our culprit doesn't."

"A few other things point to it as well. As Varn said, murder isn't Sandstone's usual work, and he's a bit old to be starting a new career. He might have just needed the proper spark to bring his true nature to life, of course, but I don't think so. It would have surfaced before now, and he'd certainly never have stayed this long in a position giving him so little scope for exercising it. I'm betting he was over the edge and brooding over his wrongs or whatever's driving him well before this opportunity for setting his private universe to rights presented itself."

She sighed but then forcibly drove the gloom from her. "Whatever about that, the information I've requested will tell us if there's been a crime in the first place and who's reponsible, Sandstone or some underling. Just be sure to stress that I want this kept very quiet until we're ready to grab the whole lot."

"I doubt I'd forget to mention that, Colonel," Karmikel told her dryly. He frowned. "It'll take time, though, Islaen, just to pull it together, much less to analyze it all."

"I know," the Commando said. "That's why I want to move on the investigation ourselves. Besides, I think I should go over it with Admiral Sithe personally."

A chill passed through her which she knew Sogan read although she was able to conceal it from Jake.

"I don't like carrying this on our own. It's too big."

The eyes of both men fell. They knew what rode on their handling of this affair and were equally uncomfortable under the burden of it.

"Let us begin, then," the Arcturian said firmly. "We will accomplish nothing further out here."

During all this time, the gurry chick had remained where she was, making no sound, but seeming to listen intently, her bright eyes darting from one to the other as each human took up the conversation. Now she flew to her place on Islaen's shoulder.

Bandit's ready.

The woman stopped short. She had forgotten the small mammal. "We can't take you with us, my little friend. You'll have to stay with Jake and the herd."

Nooo!

"You're needed here. The other humans are afraid to adopt gurries yet, in case they might accidentally hurt them. Until they do, you're the only one who can help them deal with the herd."

Bandit can only talk to you and Varn.

"You can understand the others, and you do provide a link with the goldbeasts," she pointed out. "That's enough for the time being."

The gurry gave an unhappy chirp. *Bandit likes helping the others, but you and Varn are my humans*, she wailed.

The Colonel was quiet a moment. "I don't know how much of this you're going to understand, Love, but Varn and I are sworn to serve others, and if you want to live with us, you have to be willing to do the same. We have to confront a possible renegade of our kind, and I must be able to read him as he is, not softened by you, if even a gurry can touch him. At the same time, you're needed, really and truly needed, here."

The hen-chick gave a whimper of pure misery and then took wing. *Bandit will stay,* she said as she flew off toward the camp.

Jake had watched the strange, and to him one-sided, exchange in complete amazement and now turned accusingly to his former commander.

"She looks like a martyr going off to sacrifice herself," he growled.

Islaen gave him the full account of what had passed between them. "I've never felt so guilty in my whole life," she concluded wretchedly.

Varn's laugh sounded hollow even to his own ears. "That is what we get for taking in a gurry. —Now, before more trouble arises, let us warn these people about the possibility of flooding and take our leave of them."

He sighed then and added more to himself than to either of his companions. "It will be good to be back in space again, even on such a mission as this one."

FIFTEEN

VARN WAS RIGHT about space, Islaen Connor thought as she fixed her attention for a moment on the splendor beyond the *Maid's* observation panels. All humanity's petty ugliness seemed as nothing when laid against this.

She smiled softly. If there was danger in that vast, star-studded blackness, there was also peace and an infinity of wonder for those who respected it and knew how to handle themselves within it. Travel along the starlanes was normally a pleasant experience, quiet and predictable, although emergencies could shatter that stillness with stunning abruptness.

Nothing had marred this voyage, and she had enjoyed it despite the need driving them. Now it was almost over, and with Isis' system already glistening on the distance viewer, she could feel the tension rising within her again.

The Commando sensed her husband's call and turned to give him greeting as he stepped lightly onto the bridge.

Varn Tarl Sogan was wearing the dress uniform of a Navy Captain, and her heart swelled at the sight of him. No other man she had ever known could carry a uniform as he did, and he looked more magnificent in the stark black of the Federation than he had in the Empire's scarlet.

Her pride waxed higher still as her eyes traveled to the decorations shining on his breast. There were two, each the single, brilliant star of a class one heroism citation. Most people within the huge Federation ultrasystem would never so much as see one, yet this man, in the incredibly short period of time in which he had been in active service, had earned a brace of them.

She allowed what she was feeling to pour into him and was rewarded by the slight lifting of his head. He knew she found him attractive thus and took delight in her admiration despite the fact that he would never feel completely at ease in the uniform of the ultrasystem he had fought for so many years.

He walked over to the viewer. Isis' ten planets were already visible, strung out from her like stones on one of the wire collars currently so popular on Siren. The orbits of the third and fourth were very close, as were the planets themselves, and even from here, the two looked to be very similar.

Sister worlds, he mused. *It is a wonder how they can be so superficially alike and yet be gifted so differently.*

Or be so widely apart in spirit, Islaen agreed.

Horus, the third planet, was rich in both heavy and precious minerals and was blessed with fertile soil and an abundance of free water. Set, the fourth planet, lacked all these and would never have been opened for colonization at all had it not been for her unusual synchronized orbit with her twin and the fact that she, too, was completely Terra-normal. The Federation had wanted an administrative center to service this part of the ultrasystem. The two planets provided an ideal solution, giving as they did separate bases for the military and high-priority agencies on one world and the less essential services on the other, thereby all but eliminating the congestion which plagued most other places supporting major governmental activity. As a result, both had been developed jointly.

The richest prize, the huge Navy and Stellar Patrol bases, had gone to Horus, the more favored planet of the two, but many of the civilian agencies, the Settlement Board among them, had preferred the quieter atmosphere and lack of competition for essential services offered by Set.

The woman frowned, feeling the irritation thought of the fourth planet usually aroused rise within her.

The populace had more than enough work with the spaceport, as well as supplying the needs of the organizations their world had attracted, to keep them profitably occupied, without having to throw Set open as a service station for half the vermin crawling the starlanes in this Sector. They would be fortunate if they did not pay heavily for their greed some day, and she just hoped that too many not sharing their guilt would not wind up paying along with them.

Sogan glanced once more at the screen and then settled back in his flight chair.

Strap in. I will be requesting planeting permission soon.

Will do, Admiral.

Did you contact Sandstone yet?

Aye, just before you came up. I merely asked to see him for a few minutes and assured him that our visit was entirely unofficial.

He looked at her in surprise; they had been planning to use a more forceful approach.

He agreed to see us?

Of course. I figured he would. He knows who we are. Even if he's innocent, his curiosity would drive him to meet us, and if he's guilty, he has no choice at all. He'd have no peace until he found out if we do suspect anything. After all, we saved those colonists once and got mighty stiff sentences put on the ones who wronged them. He wouldn't want to chance having the same thing happen to him.

Brilliant, Colonel.

Just another example of a Commando's naturally devious mind, Admiral.

The Arcturian brought the *Fairest Maid* down with his usual skill and went through the post-voyage check of her systems that was habit with him. That done, he set her security seals in place, and he and his companion boarded the Commando flier, which was their preferred on-world transport.

There was a sharp bite to Set's air, and he glanced inquisitively at the woman.

Close the canopy?

No. It's nippy, but the locals and long-term residents are used to it. They'd find our uniforms more than heavy enough. No use in starting off by appearing weak.

No, he agreed. *We would have the disadvantage then.*

The former Admiral braced himself so he would not cringe under the initial blast of wind as he activated the flier. It was not much to endure, he supposed, but he was still glad their journey would be a relatively short one.

This was Sogan's first visit to Set, and he looked around him curiously. He might almost have imagined that he was back on Horus save for the chill and the fact that the buildings here were fashioned of yellow rock and plastistone rather than the fine blue granite and various metals used for construction on her sister world. In the design of the structures and the layout of the port city, both planets were almost identical.

The community had been planned to function smoothly under the pressure of the heavy traffic that was part of every administrative center. The broad chief thoroughfares were flanked by huge office complexes housing the various planetary and interstellar governmental agencies. Branching off from these and fronting on smaller streets were the dwellings of those who worked in these buildings and the numerous shops and service industries providing for their needs. A number of relatively narrow, short alleys cut this formal pattern, providing quick passage between important but otherwise inefficiently widely separated locations.

He guided his vehicle into one of these last, following the instructions he had memorized before leaving the *Maid*. It was well maintained, he noted with satisfaction, quite as well as the more important routes, and was not so narrow that two large cargo transports could not have passed one another there without having to violate the pedestrian walkways, although the height of the buildings on either side made it seem quite restricted.

The towering apartments limited the amount of light reaching the street as well, and Sogan found himself frowning. He realized suddenly that he felt uneasy about this place.

He glanced swiftly at Islaen but did not attempt to link with her mind. No Commando would be happy in such a situation, and he could feel the power flowing out from her as she swept their surroundings for potential enemies. He did not wish to distract her from that work.

He shifted the control rod lightly, bringing them up a good story. Ground transport was considerably more common than airborne vehicles on Set, and this maneuver might be enough to throw off any ambush set to trap travelers.

His face hardened a little. It would be his fault if they were attacked. He had chosen to come this way instead of by the longer but more secure main highway despite the fact that Set was well known for her thugs, planet-bound pirates who preyed upon strangers and Setites alike, although the planet was not a poor one.

He comforted himself with the thought that they would soon be through the narrow place and vowed that he would not repeat this mistake on the return, maybe to their grief.

Suddenly, the Colonel's mind opened into his.

Trouble. It's hard to read individual transmissions among so many, but I can just pick up an interest in us, a predator's interest. From one of the roofs, I think.

She had linked her receptors with his, and he struggled to sort through the flood of impressions to focus on those she described.

He nodded after a moment. *I think I have them. You are right. . . .*

Sogan swerved sharply in response to her silent warning, just as a solid, yellowish object hurled past them.

Not quite past. He heard the woman gasp and felt pain radiate from her for a microsecond before she screened it. Almost at the same instant, there was the clang of something heavy striking against the flier's side.

Islaen?

A bump. It's nothing.

Even as his mind formed his question, the Arcturian glanced upward. He could see their attackers, two young men leaning over the edge of the roof, both confident of finding their victims crashed and helpless against their onslaught.

A second later, their expressions revealed first astonishment and then utter disbelief as the flier hurtled toward them. To their knowledge, the maneuver they were witnessing was physically impossible, and so it would have been by any but the Commando vehicle. No civilian craft and no other type possessed by the military could alter direction so drastically with such speed. By the time they had recovered enough from their amazement to flee, it was already on a level with them.

Islaen Connor was at the controls. Sogan had pulled her across him into his place as soon as he had sent the vehicle into its wild ascent. Her arm was still enough numbed by the blow she had taken to impair her performance in combat, and he was determined to bring down the vermin who had plotted this cowardly and totally unprovoked assault.

The two moved fast once they started to run, but Sogan's blaster was already in his hand, and he dropped the first even as he leaped from the flier onto the roof.

The second had made a quicker start. He kept his body low as he sped toward the open doorway leading into the building below.

Sogan did not fire again. He dove forward after the thug, not directly but at an angle which cut the distance between them. His body was hard, obedient to his will, and there was rage enough on him to drive it to its fullest effort. They closed, and as his quarry neared the door, he sprang.

The weight of his body bore his younger opponent to the ground. The thug did not think to surrender. He had been in tough spots before and aimed a sharp blow upward which should have ended the fight. It would have with a different opponent, but an Arcturian officer is so trained as to require no blaster or pellet gun to defend himself in personal combat. Sogan parried his arm seemingly without thought or effort even as his own fist rammed into the other's abdomen. He struck again and yet again as the ambusher doubled in agony, then went limp, his eyes glazing.

Varn, hold! No more!

Small, steel-strong fingers closed on his arm, stopping a fourth blow. *Easy, Varn. He's out of it now. You've put him in the hospital as it is.*

I would sooner send him to the mortuary, his mind muttered, but he stepped back.

He watched Islaen snap secure-cuffs on the unconscious tough.

What about the other one? he asked.

He won't be coming out of stun for a while. I cuffed him just to be sure.

Good. What do we do with them?

Throw them in the back of the flier and drop them off at Patrol headquarters. I want them shipped to Horus as soon as the medics finish with them.

Horus? he said in surprise. *You think this was planned?*

Not really, the woman replied grimly, *though this was a likely route for us to have taken. I intend to have them questioned thoroughly all the same, just in case.*

Her brown eyes glittered coldly. *They'll be charged with assaulting military personnel and, if our suspicions prove out, the indictment will be upgraded to assaulting military personnel during the course of a mission. I don't know if they'll be any wiser when they get out of prison but, by the Spirit of Space, they'll be a good deal older.*

An excellent example for the rest of their kind here, the former Admiral commented.

That, my friend, is the idea. I want to make it very clear to the scum here, and elsewhere throughout the ultrasystem, that Navy personnel are not safe targets for their preying.

A worthy motive, Colonel. At second thought, I am glad I spared them.

He tugged the torn sleeve of her uniform open, baring the flesh beneath. It was scraped in spots and already purpling, but there was no real bleeding.

What was it?

A rock, I think. We'll have a look when we go down again.

Have the medics see to that arm when we turn those two over to them.

For a bruise? Don't be ridiculous. It's not even cut.

There could be hidden damage, even a chipped bone.

No. I ran a check on myself. I can do that, remember?

Aye, but I would feel better if they were to examine you as well.

Later maybe, she promised. *Right now, we don't have the time. We'll be late getting to the Settlement Board as it is. I just hope a call from Patrol headquarters will intrigue Sandstone and not annoy him or scare him off.*

SIXTEEN

THURSTON SANDSTONE'S OFFICE was large enough to house the conferences sometimes held there and so decorated as to seem comfortable and reassuring to the Settlement Board's clients, who were the most frequent extra-agency visitors to it. The walls were sheathed in a beige, coarsely-woven fabric and were broken by two doors and by a large window overlooking Set's capital. Several good near-space views of various planets and planetary systems graced the walls.

The furniture was solid and attractively neutral. It was large in scale, and the couch and the several chairs were all obviously well able to take the weight and bulk of the largest prospective colonist.

Sandstone himself was not an impressive figure. He was tall enough but quite slender, almost frail-looking. His northern Terran blood was apparent in the thin face, and his well-modulated voice carried the accent of his homeworld. His hair was perceptibly thinning, proof that he had not availed himself of any of the readily available treatments to prevent or reverse that condition.

His eyes were a nondescript gray and seemed always to be on one, piercing and prying, but they would never stay to meet any return challenge. Islaen found them strange enough to give her a feeling of unease whenever she felt them touch her.

That he was a nervous man was apparent from the twitch which occasionally tugged at the corners of his mouth and the constant movement of the long fingers.

He is not one to inspire great confidence, Varn's mind remarked.

Nor great fear either, his companion reflected, hoping as she did that their suspicions were wrong. She sensed that there was or had been at least the potential for good and maybe for greatness in the Settlement Agent, and if it had been warped, then she was witness to a true tragedy.

Be that as it may, she had her own part to play, to discover the truth and to prevent a major disaster if the fear which had brought her to Set was fact.

The two officers were seated in chairs drawn up beside Sandstone's in a conversational setting rather than before his desk as they had anticipated.

The woman now smiled apologetically. "We owe you our thanks twice over, Mr. Sandstone, both for seeing us on such short notice and then for pardoning our delay."

"Say no more, Colonel Connor. I must confess that I leaped at the chance to meet you and Captain Sogan after all I had heard about your deeds on Visnu. As for your coming late, that obviously couldn't be helped. You said you'd been assaulted, I believe, when you called from Patrol headquarters."

"Aye, to our attackers' sorrow."

She gave him a quick account of what had occurred.

His expression darkened. "Young villains! Their kind is a blight on the entire ultrasystem and on Set herself. She would be a fine planet without them."

Sandstone scowled furiously. "Sometimes I think the whole native populace should be resettled individually on space rocks where all their energies would have to be directed to stark survival."

He caught himself. "That sounds terrible, doesn't it, but decent Setites and we long-term residents get so sick of this sort of thing. I'm glad you two were able to put an end to their game anyway."

She smiled again. "So were we, Mr. Sandstone. We didn't enjoy finding ourselves their targets."

"No, I suppose not. You didn't kill them, though?"

"That wasn't necessary."

"Of course not. Of course not. —You say you had them sent to Horus?"

Islaen Connor stiffened inwardly. Until this point, the Terran had been radiating anger. Now, he was suspicious.

Her companion had remained quiet thus far, but he nodded in answer to this.

"Aye. They are worthless in themselves, but they can serve as an example of what will happen to others of their ilk who imagine they can prey on Navy personnel."

No Federation-born officer could have spoken thus, put that tone into his voice and carried it successfully, but the Arcturian had in that moment become again the man she had first known, Varn Tarl Sogan, war prince and blood kin to the Emperor himself, the absolute ruler of entire star systems in peace and commander of a full invasion fleet in war.

The power and authority he radiated were his in truth, bred into him and into his line for more centuries than a great many well-established planets had been settled, and Sandstone reacted instinctively to it. He straightened himself as if one much superior had suddenly come into his presence.

"They'll at least be serving some useful purpose, then, Sir," Sandstone replied respectfully, his doubts momentarily forgotten.

Bless you, Varn, her mind whispered gratefully.

She hastened to add her own agreement. "That's the way we figured it. Sort of a payment for the trouble to which they put us."

The woman shrugged then, as if dismissing the subject from her mind. "That's over with now. We had more important reasons for wanting to see you than discussing Set's low-life."

"Aye, of course, Colonel Connor. You mentioned you had some questions about the colony on Jade of Kuan Yin."

"We do. In fact, we just left there specifically to see you."

His brows lifted at that, and she could feel the tension rising in him, but the Commando went on smoothly.

"We have an interest in the settlement, as you can well imagine, and we went to Jade for a brief furlough. We'd scarcely planeted before we learned that those people intend to become nomads." She grimaced. "That gave us a start, sure enough, especially when their liaison officer, who's a close friend of ours, as you probably know, tells us that you yourself proposed a sensible settled life in that rich plain where they're camped at the moment. If there's some solid reason behind such a seemingly ridiculous decision, I'd appreciate knowing it—if you're at liberty to discuss it, of course."

He gave her a meaningful look. "Why didn't you ask the Amonites directly?"

Sogan's lips curved into a smile. It did not reach his eyes, but the other did not notice that. "They do not respond well to questioning. They have some reason to trust us, and they made us very welcome, but still, one does not press them for detail they do not volunteer of themselves."

"You're entirely right, Captain. It was a stupid question to ask. No one should know those people better than I."

His voice took on an irritable note. "They're really a very ungrateful folk. Totally unappreciative of the efforts being made in their behalf. After all, they did try to circumvent the Settlement Board originally. I know they suffered for it, but they should still be glad to be in competent hands now and listen when a studied plan is presented to them."

"Then there is no concrete reason for their choosing a nomadic life-style?" Islaen persisted.

"None whatsoever, Colonel! It was just some baseless whim of theirs. In fact, I rather lost my temper when they remained adamant in it, I'm ashamed to say. Mr. Karmikel probably mentioned it to you."

"He did, I think, but your annoyance is certainly understandable. —I apologize for having troubled you with my questions and worries, but I was hoping you could give me some sensible explanation, possibly some previously mentioned alternative rejected by yourself but pleasing to them. That would've set my mind at rest."

"I'm sorry there, Colonel. There simply isn't one, at least not to a non-Amonite mind."

She shook her head, as if in disgust. "This must all be very disappointing for you, Mr. Sandstone. I understand you Settlement Board people put a great deal of time and thought into your proposals."

"We do."

He paused. "Would you care to see some of my suggestions, the final one and some of the alternatives you were right in imagining I developed?" he asked them rather eagerly. "I cleared my calendar in preparation for your visit and so have the afternoon free to go over them with you. If you have the time, that is," he added apologetically.

"We most certainly do!" the Noreenan replied. "This is a great deal more than we expected, Mr. Sandstone."

With a deal more behind it than words or voice would seem to indicate.

A touch from Varn's mind confirmed that opinion. She had linked her receptors with him at the beginning of the interview, and the former Admiral agreed full well with her that a stronger motive than the desire to display undervalued labor to a sympathetic audience was at work in their host.

Thurston Sandstone rose to his feet. "Excellent! I'll begin gathering everything together at once."

He glanced at the interbuilding communicator on his desk. "It'll take time to dig it all out of the holding files, I'm afraid, so if I may make a suggestion . . . Indeed, I'll be so bold as to issue an order, Colonel. I notice you're favoring your arm a bit. We have a small but quite fine medical staff here, on the next level up, and I want our doctor to see you and run a renewer over you if he thinks it a good idea. —Please, Colonel Connor. I'd really feel better for knowing you had the proper care. It's silly maybe, but I feel a little responsible that you were hurt coming to see me."

"I have been pressing her to look after it myself, Mr. Sandstone," the Arcturian said quickly. "Come, Colonel," he added, "I think you had best surrender. The odds are against you in this."

His thought touched hers. *Play along with him, Islaen. Let us see what he intends.*

Will do. I'm curious, too.

She laughed and raised her hands in an exaggerated gesture of capitulation. "I yield! It's nothing but a bad bump really, but I don't want to be an ungracious guest. Tell your doctor we're on our way."

SEVENTEEN

IT WAS LATE afternoon before the off-worlders finally left the Settlement Agent's office once more. They hurried to their flier, but Sogan slowed his pace when they actually came within sight of it.

Islaen matched her steps to his. She said nothing while he scanned the machine, giving it a quick and unobtrusive but surprisingly thorough visual inspection.

Everything seems all right, he declared after a few seconds.

You don't think he'd try anything that obvious? It'd draw too much attention down on him since we've only just left his office.

I prefer to depend on my own senses rather than what should be reasonable when it comes to a potential ambush, the man answered tightly.

He gave a sigh of relief as he slid behind the controls. *It will be good to get back to the* Maid.

That it will, she agreed.

The Commando restrained her urge to smile as she glanced at him. Varn Tarl Sogan was about the only one she knew who did not loosen the high, tight collar of his dress uniform the moment the need for wearing it was past. She had opened hers as soon as they had quit the building.

He felt her eyes on him. *An interesting day,* he commented. *What do you think?*

We have a case.

You are sure? I detected no feeling of guilt, not even when Sandstone acknowledged the Amonites' sufferings.

I'm not assuming a competent conscience. —No, there wasn't any direct evidence of a crime, but he was nervous with us, suspicious beyond any need on an innocent man.

He was truly angry with those thugs, he said thoughtfully.

Aye, but he was angry nearly all the time to some degree.

She stared through the windshield for a moment without actually seeing the road before them.

By all the old gods, Varn, I've never experienced hostility like that before. Its focus and manifestation may have altered, but it never left him at all. Someone ridden like that could kill very readily if he were provoked enough.

She shivered. *I wish I knew what "enough" would be.*

If he is mad, it could be just about anything. Sogan frowned. *We do not even know that. With the renegade bull, there was no doubt, but that is not true with him.*

Insanity takes many forms, I suppose. It hasn't swept his reason and personality completely the way it did with the poor goldbeast. It's more like an insidious infection with Sandstone, hidden and pernicious.

An apt description, I fear. If we are correct. We are no psychomedics to make such a diagnosis.

No, but everything inside me tells me we're right and even more right to push this.

You will see Ram Sithe when we get back to Horus?

She nodded. *I will. We need his backing. Luckily, my hunches have paid off well enough in the past that he's likely to give it.*

The planeting field was before them by then, and the Arcturian increased speed a little as he made for the small-vessel docking bays, which comprised the bulk of the port's facilities. Most of the really big ships and all of the transgalactics coming into Isis' system planeted on Horus.

Set's spaceport was a busy place despite that, and they traveled for another ten minutes before the *Fairest Maid* at last came into view.

Sogan's heart swelled at the sight of her. A slender, tall, silver spire glistening gloriously in the sun-star's light, she seemed more vision than reality, the embodiment of all a starship should be or had come to be in human hearts and minds.

His love for his ship did not prevent him from studying her even more critically than he had the flier.

Suddenly, his right hand dropped from the controls to close over Islaen's arm. *Someone has been at her!*

What! I don't see anything. . . .

He brought the vehicle to a halt. *Her hatch is not sitting right. —Come on, but take care. We do not want to walk into any surprises.*

No one's here now, she said tightly.

That could be quite irrelevant, she thought as she stepped out of the flier. Those who set booby traps rarely waited around to watch them activate. . . .

She saw what had disturbed her companion. Sogan, with his passionate desire for security, always kept the *Maid*'s hatch closc to space sealed whenever he left her. The locks were not that tight now. The difference was almost infinitesimal, but a spacer knew his ship better than his own body, and he had spotted the change at once.

He got out and came around the flier to join her. *You see it?*

I do. —Stay back, and get out of line with the hatch in case it blows. This is my work.

Sogan obeyed although he allowed her to feel his dislike for sending her into a peril he himself did not share. Too much was riding on them to risk both unnecessarily, and a Commando could rival many a demolitions expert in the setting and disarming of explosives.

Islaen Connor's pulse was racing frantically as she mounted the boarding ramp. She did not pause until she reached the hatch. Here, she came to a complete stop and stood before it looking at it intently for several seconds, then she knelt and examined it minutely. Few in all the ultrasystem knew better than she how many unlikely forms a deadly charge could bear and how readily one could be concealed.

No sign of anything. The tension ebbed from her, but the guerrilla went through her examination a second time. Still nothing.

Stceling herself, she loosened the disturbed locks and drew back the hatch to reveal a second barrier inside. This, too, she studied with great care.

At last, she straightened. *It looks all right. They got through the ship's locks, but they didn't manage the antipersonnel seals or voice locks.*

The intruders—or intruder—probably had a considerable shock when they found them, she thought. Neither were standard equipment on anything smaller than a battle cruiser and were unheard of on a vessel of the *Maid*'s class.

One more test remained. The woman gingerly released the starship's defenses and slid the inner hatch open.

Her eyes closed in relief. They were there, two tiny, intricately entwined strands of spider silk, each one so fine as to be well-nigh invisible. She used to feel embarrassed whenever her husband set this warning, deeming it a bare step from active paranoia. Now she blessed him for his care.

All clear, Varn!

He joined her in the next moment. *I go in first, just in case.*

They found nothing amiss within, and soon both were on the bridge.

Varn Tarl Sogan set the tape reader he had brought up with him from the crew's cabin on the broad shelf formed by the instrument panel.

The Commando officer took a spool capsule from one of the several recorders installed there and handed it to him.

Let's see if we got any pretty pictures. Our uninvited visitors shouldn't have expected this, either.

He nodded. Any tampering with the hatch activated the mechanism. Unless they had been badly outsmarted by an extraordinarily capable and well-equipped technician, they should have a record of the better part of the attempted break-in.

The screen flickered, then the picture stabilized. The perspective was oddly distorted since the lens had been fixed directly above the culprits, but both figures were fully recognizable.

Sandstone, Sogan hissed. *Do you know the one with him?*

She shook her head. *No, but he's a tough-looking character, a space mongrel, I'd say. I can't see any particular racial type in him.*

The stranger was a much bigger man than the Settlement Agent, with a hard face and a murky complexion. He obviously knew his way around starships, and some of the tools he removed from the satchel casually slung from his broad shoulders would have drawn most unfavorable interest from the Stellar Patrol.

He was not long in springing the outer hatch but drew back with a strong oath after working for a few seconds on the inner one.

He turned on Sandstone and declared that not only could he not manage the guards on this ship but that he would not mess with anyone entitled to carry them, that he did not intend to be drawn into anything that big, not before they were ready to make their own move. After that, he sealed the outer hatch again in what he believed to be its original position and hastened down the ramp, leaving his companion to follow after, lugging the small, apparently heavy package he had been holding.

The screen went blank again.

The cur, Islaen muttered. *That's why he made it so damned nearly impossible for us to refuse his offer to go over those plans. He must have nipped over here while we were at medical or waiting for his files. The journey's more than short enough for that.*

Of course that is when he did it. We knew he was up to something. Now we know what, but it is the why of it that is important. —I wonder what he had in that box. He was handling it gently enough.

Maybe something to try to read our records or to foul our navputer. Maybe something to blow us and the Maid *to atoms, probably when we were spaceborne once more.*

She looked at the blank reader. *We have him at least.*

Not for what we want.

No, but burglarizing a Navy vessel is a serious offense, and it'll be espionage if we class this jaunt as a mission. He'll face a military tribunal for it in either case, which'll give us a better chance of keeping the involvement of the river tears under security wraps. If nothing else, he'll be forced to undergo psychotesting. That should bring out the rest even if we can't introduce it or try him directly. If it's like we think, he'll be put where he can't do more harm or leak the news to avenge himself.

There should be no question of his guilt now. Nothing else would explain this attempt. It is no fear of having an error betrayed, not if he came in such company as his comrade seems to be, one whose comment about their own plans proclaims an on-going relationship.

You don't have to convince me, Varn. I'm all too well aware of that.

He looked at her sharply. There was a new note in that thought, a fear, almost a despair.

Islaen, what is it?

I may have made a disastrous move in coming to Set.

She pressed her hands to her eyes, as she often did when troubled. *Our visit must've scared the starlight out of Sandstone to drive him to this at all, much less move him to bring his cohort openly with him.*

That was before we went over his files, he reminded her. *Your sympathy and praise calmed him considerably.*

Aye, I may have played him well enough to allay his suspicions, but I'm wondering whether he'll be able to ease his bullyboy's as readily. That one's not going to like our sudden appearance any more than Sandstone did at first, and he's not going to forget the Maid's *security system. He could well believe we're here on an active investigation with a fix on them.*

Her eyes were as bleak as the cold of deep space when she raised them to his.

By the Spirit ruling all space, Varn, I hope I haven't precipitated the very disaster we're trying to prevent.

EIGHTEEN

ADMIRAL RAM SITHE of the Federation Navy stood before the huge star map covering the whole of one wall in his otherwise plain office. He was a relatively small man, typical in body and feature of his south Terran subrace, but there was that in him, an aura of command, a presence, which filled the moderately large room.

He turned at last to face the woman seated before his desk. His expression was grave; his dark, normally marvelously expressive eyes were inscrutable.

"You were able to come up with no solid evidence at all, Colonel?"

"Nothing, Admiral Sithe, except for the attempt to breach the *Maid*'s defenses. There can be no denying that, however."

"No, there can't. It will get a conviction against Thurston Sandstone or force medical confinement as the circumstances dictate, but I wonder if that will be enough for you."

Islaen Connor met his penetrating eyes steadily. "If he's guilty of the betrayal I envision, or if he's so base a coward as to try to conceal an error of this magnitude while leaving those people in danger, then, aye, I want vengeance, and I want it badly."

"You may have to forget about it if you intend to keep the presence of the river tears a secret even though you'll be dealing with a military tribunal rather than a civilian court. For my part, I think that must be your first priority."

"Of course, it must!" she answered a bit hotly. "Do you imagine me such a child that I'd put my own whims before that? If the peril to the Amonites can be averted and Sandstone's fangs drawn so he can't cause them or anyone else harm, I'll be more than satisfied."

The man smiled. "Peace, Colonel. I merely wished to hear you affirm what I already knew. Rest easy on that score. Captain Sogan's security precautions will assure us this much of a victory."

His tone became harder. "You say Sandstone went over some alternate plans with you. Was there anything wrong with them?"

She shook her head. "Nothing I could spot at first glance, but I didn't imagine there would be. One potential disaster could be an error, but not several. The suggestions were merely not attractive enough to move the settlers to adopt them. As it turned out, they came up with their own idea and spoiled everything for him."

Sithe fixed his eyes on the map for a moment before bringing his attention back to her.

"We could move against him now, but I believe you're right in wanting to wait until we can round up the whole lot."

"Just don't wait too long, Sir." Islaen told him of her fear that her visit might push Sandstone's pirates out of their passive state.

"I figured he'd want to deal with us himself. I certainly never imagined he'd draw his butchers in on it, and I'm not at all sure how they'll react to us. We're not Patrol, but they're still bound not to like our sudden appearance."

"You are not guilty of the kind of cowardice you've imagined as possible for Sandstone," the man observed.

She only frowned. "I've made mistakes before but none as potentially costly as this one."

"We're running a check on Sandstone's unsavory-looking friend. That should give us a lead on the others in his circle and help us keep tabs on them. As for the rest, you made a reasonable decision as to a course of action, one I should not only have condoned but would probably have commanded you to undertake had the decision been mine, so stop heaping guilt on yourself. You have more than enough concrete problems to keep you occupied."

"That I surely have, Sir," she replied ruefully.

Islaen relaxed a little. With Sithe behind her, her fight in Jade's cause was suddenly both less difficult and far less lonely.

"What about those two thugs we shipped off to you?" she asked. "Were they involved or merely free agents?"

"The latter. They're nothing but a couple of vicious young roughs with lamentably poor judgment when it comes to choosing victims."

"I hope when word of what's happened to them gets around, it'll put the fear of the old gods on a few of their pals."

"It might. We're allowing it to circulate for that purpose. Some of Set's lesser lights have been growing far too daring of late."

Sithe's tone hardened again. "We almost didn't get to question the one Sogan tackled at all. It took two major sessions under regrowth to set him to rights."

Islaen Connor only shrugged. "Varn showed considerable restraint. An Arcturian officer could smash every organ in a man's belly with three blows like he got in if he chose to use them that way, and he didn't hurt the first one at all."

"I have to admit it surprised me that he elected to stun rather than burn him."

"That was always his way. Varn never killed unnecessarily, even in anger."

The Admiral nodded, then gave her a sharp look. "How is he doing?"

"His actions on and over Astarte should answer that, Sir," she replied in surprise.

"I've never doubted Captain Sogan's skill or his courage, Colonel, or his willingness to exercise them when the need presents itself, but I did put my head right on the block when I commissioned him and then sharpened the axe by authorizing the outfitting of his ship as I did. Since my striving after perfection has still left me a good few degrees short of omniscience, I feel better for having a bit of reassurance now and then."

Her head raised. "Varn Tarl Sogan gave his oath by his own

wish and will, and he'll hold to that oath while any spark of life remains in him."

Her eyes flashed. "He is a war prince. What happened to him hasn't changed that."

Ram Sithe turned away from her, and she became aware of a sadness radiating from him.

She leaned forward. "Is something wrong, Sir?"

"Wrong? No, not wrong," he answered after a moment, surprised that she had detected so much; he was accustomed to concealing his inner feelings and knew he had not been careless on this occasion.

He decided to answer the Commando truthfully. "I suppose I empathize with the man a little. My own people are an old race, strong in tradition, and I am one of our ancient royalty. I can't help but wonder how I should have reacted had fate dealt with me as it did with Varn Tarl Sogan."

"You would have done well, Sir," Islaen responded quietly. "You're alike in a great many ways, enough so for me to be able to answer that with complete certainty."

The Terran smiled. "Fortune has made him some recompense in teaming him with you, Colonel Connor."

He straightened. "Captain Sogan did not accompany you here?"

"No, Sir. He prefers to remain with the *Maid,* especially after that business on Set."

"And he prefers to avoid me, perhaps? He once held a higher rank than mine. Now, he is much less and is in my debt besides."

The Commando-Colonel looked at him sharply. Ram Sithe had the reputation for an almost uncanny ability to read the motives of those with whom he dealt, and she found it disconcerting to have it turned on her or, through her, on Varn. Quite independently of her will, her mind shields snapped into place although she realized full well that no probe was being sent out against her.

She forced herself to steady. "Possibly," she answered candidly, "Particularly since he has always held you in great respect. Chiefly, however, he has simply learned it's wiser to keep a very low profile when in port."

She described the incident that had marred their last visit to Horus.

The Admiral was frowning darkly by the time she had

finished her tale. "It's a poor testament to Federation peoples, but I fear Sogan's right."

"He hasn't made the *Fairest Maid* a coward's prison, Sir." She touched the tiny communicator on her wrist. "If you'd like, I'll bring him here now."

"No. If I need to see Captain Sogan, I can very well come to him."

He shook his head. "You certainly have found a most complicated life for yourself, Colonel."

The Noreenan laughed. "It's one that suits us both despite a few decided drawbacks."

His smile answered hers. "I don't doubt that in the least."

Sithe studied the Commando-Colonel with a new attention, although he took care to exercise the controls he had learned and practiced from his early youth to prevent his thoughts or emotions from rising beyond his innermost mind. This woman had displayed an amazing sensitivity to his mood earlier, and he did not like the idea that he might have been telegraphing himself to her like an undisciplined novice whose face showed his every thought.

The slight unease she had put on him did not lessen either the sympathy or the admiration he felt for her. It was a heavy burden that she was bearing, too heavy for most, but Islaen Connor had been used to carrying responsibility of frightening magnitude since her late girlhood. If anyone could endure it, she would.

The regret he often felt when in the presence of his officers rose up within him. It was wrong, basically, utterly wrong, that so much strength, so much ability, had to find its flowering in the cruel madness of war. This woman's life should have been a most different one. She should have spent these years ranging the starlanes, exploring and maybe discovering planets, interacting with their inhabitants, intelligent and nonintelligent alike, not engaged in deadly battle, ever under the almost constant shadow of dire peril to herself and others.

He sighed in his heart. Only a coward or a fool wasted energy railing against the unalterable courses laid out by fate, the paths ordained for each individual by the Spirit ruling space.

He, too, had his work before him, work this Commando had given him.

"You and Captain Sogan return to Jade for now and await

further developments. We have most of the explorers' notes in and have begun checking them against the official reports. Once we have anything, I'll let you know."

"Thank you, Sir. What story are you using to explain our wanting all this information?" she added curiously.

"That we want to do a comparison of planetary conditions." His black eyes sparkled. "In a certain sense, there's truth in that."

The woman laughed. "In a certain sense. —Thank you again, Admiral. We'll be waiting at the Amonite camp for your report."

She sobered suddenly. "I don't have to tell you that I'd rather be wrong about all this."

"I hope you are as well, Colonel Connor, but I think we are both too much realists to imagine that you are."

NINETEEN

BOTH VARN AND Islaen were in much brighter spirits when they lifted from Horus than they had been when planeting there, and they made the journey back to Kuan Yin's system in what seemed like no time at all.

The Arcturian kept their speed high when they took to the flier once more after reaching Jade's surface, and it was not too many hours before they left the last of the hill country behind and entered upon the potentially death-shadowed plain.

Islaen looked about her. It was evening, and the sun-star cast a soft, lovely glow over all the world around them.

Everything seems so perfectly peaceful, she said with a little sigh. *It's hard to believe nature or humanity could change it all so drastically in a few minutes.*

We are forewarned now. With luck, any such changes should leave no one the worse.

Except the perpetrators in the latter event, I sincerely hope.

Sogan glanced at the woman as she shifted restlessly in the seat beside him. *It has been several hours since we last stopped. Would you like to stretch your legs for a while?*

No, not unless you're starting to get a bit tired. We're near enough to the camp that I'm anxious to push on and reach it.

She colored slightly. *I miss Bandit.*

He laughed. *I thought that had something to do with it.*

You're not exactly immune to that desire yourself, Varn Tarl Sogan! the guerrilla retorted hotly, then she, too, laughed. *What a pair we are, fretting over an absent gurry!*

I wonder if she has any like feeling for us, he mused a trifle sadly.

She was wretched when we left.

We don't know how long feeling or memory last with these little creatures.

Her face fell but brightened again in the next moment, warmed by anger.

Bandit has not forgotten us!

As if to confirm her statement, a rush of emotion pierced their minds in that moment. Both gasped in amazement at the clarity of it and because a transmission of such strength could be pouring from the tiny body which only then hurtled into their sight.

For the next several seconds, there was no coherent thought in the sending, just an infinity of joy and relief.

Bandit reached them and whirled around them so closely and with such wild abandon that they were forced to shut their eyes several times for fear that she might sideswipe them with a madly flickering wing.

The woman kept talking to her, and finally she calmed enough to settle into Islaen's outstretched palm.

The chick was trembling violently, and her heart was racing so rapidly that it was nearly impossible to detect any individual beat.

The woman put everything she could summon of affection and reassurance into both her voice and the transmissions of her mind as she caressed the Jadite hen.

Sogan bent over her as well. He was thoroughly alarmed by the magnitude of Bandit's agitation and gave to her even as did his wife, to a degree that surprised Islaen. She had not known he could open himself like this, much less that he could permit himself to do so even for so wonderful a little creature as the gurry.

Islaen . . . Varn . . .

"It's all right, Love," she whispered. "We're back now."

Don't leave Bandit again. Ever.

She raised her head to look at them, and the Commando felt her throat tighten. The chick's feathers were wet with tears.

Animals capable of crying were common to the universe. Nearly every planet including Terra had at least two or three species that did, but this was her own gurry, and she was responsible for her misery.

The man was equally affected, and he reached out timidly to stroke her, as if he believed rejection of his touch would be only just.

"Never again by our wills, Small One," he promised.

Bandit was worried. All the time, I was worried.

"We're safe now, Little Love," Islaen Connor assured her, "for the time being at least."

Yes, but stay with Bandit. You are Bandit's humans. I must take care of you.

The off-worlders started. They had seen the gurries' relationship with the goldbeasts, and now with them, as one in which the fliers received comfort and protection in exchange for the goodwill they projected and, unconsciously, for the way they facilitated rapid communication throughout the herd. Apparently, the small mammals saw it differently. Islaen remembered suddenly that the hen had mentioned that her kind acted as scouts when a renegade had been driven out from the herd and was lurking, a potential threat, in the hill country. That service must be more important than she had originally imagined, and maybe it was only one of many rendered by the gurries. There was indeed an enormous amount to be learned about the life native to Jade of Kuan Yin.

"We can't stay, Bandit," she said firmly, speaking as if to another human because she did not know how to simplify her words to a greater degree, "but where we go, you go unless the Amonites expressly forbid us to take you."

Bandit will go! I won't stay without you.

"It won't come to that," she answered hastily. "They'll have gurries of their own by then and will know how much this means to you."

Good.

The chick was tired after so much speech and such an excess of emotion. She snuggled down, letting her head rest against the gently curving fingers.

The Noreenan woman smiled at her. "I brought something for you."

Immediately, the small head raised again, and Bandit gave an excited whistle.

Food?

"Not exactly."

She fumbled in one of her belt pouches and withdrew a package from it. Opening this carefully, she took out a flake of some brown substance.

"This is genuine Terran milk chocolate. I grated it up nice and small for you before we planeted. Don't gulp it down. Just take your time and let it melt on your tongue."

Unappetizing as it looked, the chick pecked at it. She looked inquiringly at Islaen for a moment, then suddenly burst into a purring whistle.

More! she demanded in great excitement.

The woman laughed. "Later. Like I said, it's not food but what humans call a treat. We'll have more after we eat tonight."

Varn shook his head in mock disgust. *We will get no peace from her now. When did you find time to buy it?*

While you were fueling the Maid. *There's a big sweet shop at the port. I wanted her to taste something besides rations,* she added defensively.

She scowled at his answering laugh. *I did get some for us, too.*

The Commando opened her jacket so that Bandit could curl inside it out of the rising evening chill.

Let's go, Varn. Jake'll be anxious to hear our report.

It was well into the night before the two off-worlders and their gurry at last found themselves alone in their caravan and at liberty to take their rest. Islaen leaned back against the couch, closing her eyes and resting her head against its top edge.

I'm absolutely spent. It's been one busy day, even if it held no emergencies to enliven it.

Sogan made her no answer, and she looked at him.

He was sitting in the chair across the narrow room from her, his head down, gazing into some place invisible to her. She realized he had been quiet, withdrawn, ever since they had reached the encampment, and she spoke his name aloud to gain his attention.

He looked up. *Sorry. I was thinking.*

Could I help? she inquired gently.

He sighed. *I was wondering about these gurries, wondering*

what they are and what their contact with our species may mean for them.

They are themselves, whatever that may be, the woman answered slowly. *As for the rest, only the Spirit of Space knows. One thing for sure, they're lucky it's this bunch who found them. Amonites may prefer their own, but it's because they like their own ways and not because they imagine they're basically superior to any other planet's offspring.*

I know. They even tolerate a wandering Arcturian.

To her surprise, he shuddered and turned away.

Varn . . .

I was just thinking what might, what would have happened had my kind discovered them, the evil that we—that I myself—would have wrought had we learned what they were, never even recognizing that it was evil at all. . . .

The anguish on him ripped into her, and a new fear rose up in her.

You're not ashamed of what you are, Varn? she whispered, hardly daring to ask such a question of him.

The former Admiral did not appear to resent it. He rallied himself.

Ashamed? No, not that. There is too much worthy of pride in us, but we are wrong as well, wrong in so many ways.

Sogan gave her a tired smile. *Come, my Islaen. It is late, and I, too, am weary. We shall both be the better for a night's sleep.*

Islaen Connor's eyes opened as the communicator on her wrist buzzed for her attention.

"Jake, are you out of your mind?" she demanded in no good humor. "It's 4:34 in the morning. . . ."

"Sorry, Colonel, but Admiral Sithe's calling on the interstellar transceiver. He's on scramble and will talk only to you."

The Commando hurried into enough of her clothes to be able to show herself publicly and raced for the caravan housing the camp's major communications equipment.

Sogan came with her but waited outside with Jake Karmikel during the long minutes while she was in conference with Ram Sithe.

Islaen rejoined them at last. Her back was straight, her face fixed, determined, and it required no reading of her thought for them to know that the news she had received was grave and probably very ill.

She wasted no time. "The studies we wanted are complete, and it's exactly as we thought. Thurston Sandstone's under arrest right now."

"What about the others?" the Arcturian demanded.

"Escaped, or, rather, they were already gone when our people started looking for them. I guess our ship-burglar decided not to take any chances and lifted as soon as he could round up his crew and get off-world." Her mouth tightened. "He has good reason for wanting to avoid any brush with Federation authorities."

"A pirate?" Jake asked.

"A captain of command rank in the biggest fleet still operating in the Sector. They haven't troubled this quadrant much since their ships planet on Set now and then, and they like to keep a low profile, but I guess this was too big and too easy to resist, especially since they would be able to grab the stones without ever revealing they had been the ones to take them had everything worked out as planned."

"And they have all the power they need to pull off a direct raid." That was a statement. The former Commando knew full well what a large pirate fleet was capable of accomplishing against a colony planet defended only by the weapons banks of a single spaceport.

She gave a cold laugh. "They might as well be an Arcturian invasion fleet for all Jade can do against them, especially if they could come in by surprise, before the port could bring her defenses to ready. Even with forewarning, a few ships could keep the gunners there busy while others come in to take the river tears and wipe out any colonists too close to the scene. They need remove only one deposit to make the venture a fabulously profitable one."

"I trust the Navy's on its way?"

"Aye, but even fighters need time to get here. Until they do, it's up to us. —Help me rouse the camp. We don't know when the attack's coming, or that there's really one on its way at all for that matter, but we must assume that those pirates'll be hitting us hard and hitting very soon."

Commando-Colonel Islaen Connor had faced these people once before bearing the tidings of impending doom. They had heard her quietly then, calmly, but not so now.

That which had threatened them on Visnu had been an almost primal force, a well-nigh mindless insect horde whose coming would have spelled terrible, inevitable death for anyone caught in its advance but which carried no taint of guilt or blame.

This was something very different, the brutal plotting of a twisted and greedy man, a being who knew them and had worked closely with them and could yet send them and their children to almost unavoidable destruction.

Angry and bitter words rang out on every side, against Sandstone and his hirelings and also against the Federation which had appointed him, the ultrasystem whose vast impersonality no offspring of Amon would ever like or ever be able to trust.

Islaen let them go on for some seconds, knowing the shock this betrayal was for them, but she was not about to permit them to grow wild.

"Quiet!" she snapped, and the authority on her, that and the respect with which they held her, was such that near silence fell upon the crowd.

"Varn, Jake, and I all represent the Federation, too. We laid our lives out for you once and are prepared to do it again, as we might very well have to do if the Navy doesn't get here fast."

Gaea of Amon seized upon her words. Clear thought and sensible planning would deliver her people out of this. Panic and mob behavior most assuredly would not.

"What would you have us do?" she asked.

"You can't stay here, not until we know exactly what those pirates' plans are.

"Leave at once. Send most of the populace and supplies on ahead. Volunteers will remain with the caravans and travel a good day or more behind and along a slightly different path. If you are followed despite everything and traced, it's on the wagons that the attack will be centered then, allowing the most of you to make your escape."

She glanced out beyond the Amonites encircling her.

"The herd must go, too. It would be criminal to permit innocent beasts to suffer harm because humans can't control their greed. These, and certainly the gurries, have shown themselves to possess a sensitivity more approaching our own than our definition of an animal's. To let them be slaughtered would amount, morally, to murder."

"Will they move?"

"Aye, or I believe so. They understand the concept of renegades, remember. You'll have to make haste and adopt chicks, however. One channel won't be sufficient since it'll probably be necessary and maybe essential for both the main party and the decoys to communicate with the goldbeasts while you're on the run."

"What will you three do?" Gaea inquired.

"Jake'll accompany you, of course. Varn and I must get back to the port and warn it against potential attack. I don't want to do that from here."

Her eyes flickered to the Arcturian. "Besides, the *Maid* will have to maintain the watch until help arrives."

Sogan nodded. "I left her space-ready. We can lift as soon as we board."

The Councilwoman felt some of the tension leave her. They were competent, able, these ones, sure of themselves and both trained and equipped to thwart the men of violence ranged against them. She might neither be able to comprehend nor condone a lifeway dedicated to war work, but these three, warriors though they be, had given themselves to the service of the innocent and otherwise helpless folk who formed the bulk of the ultrasystem's populace, and for the second time in her life, she gave solemn and fervent thanks for their presence and for their interest in her colony.

"We should move away from the herd entirely?" she asked almost casually.

"No. Travel with it. The goldbeasts may even carry you on their backs if you request it, the children at least. So few can hide from most instruments amongst so many living things."

"How long shall we remain in hiding?"

"We'll let you know. I'll transmit on one of the Commando frequencies and prefix my call with a code sequence I'll give you in a minute. Obey no order not arriving on that wave or without that opening."

TWENTY

LITTLE MORE REMAINED to be said, and once those final commands were given, Islaen hastened toward her flier.

She was as easy in her mind as it was possible to be under these circumstances. The Amonites' basic discipline and practical good sense had stood by them on Visnu and would serve them as well on Jade of Kuan Yin. She no more doubted that than she doubted their courage and determination. They would follow her orders and Jake's later on as the situation developed, and if anything went amiss, it would be through her own failure or fortune's ill willing. She could ask or do no more at this point.

A small, feathered form streaked into the machine ahead of her. "No, Love. Stay with the herd or with Jake. We could be going into danger."

Nooo! Bandit goes with you. Islaen promised!

Varn joined them. He linked his mind with the gurry and then with his consort. *Yield, Colonel. She loves you.*

But this isn't like setting goldbeasts against amphibians! We mightn't be able to protect her, or ourselves either, for that matter!

She is aware of that and would still go. Gurries do not separate from their partners once adoption takes place, and the fact that we are human appears not to alter that. —Come. We have no time to waste arguing.

Very well, the woman agreed reluctantly. *Settle in, both of you.*

She sighed at the chick's contented whistle. "I only hope your love for us doesn't cost you heavily, little friend."

Sogan took the controls. Such was his skill with vehicles, with machinery of any kind, that Islaen had surrendered that task to him almost from the beginning of their relationship, and by now he was as familiar with the Commando flier as he was with the bridge of the *Fairest Maid*. He went fairly high, though not enough so as to draw attention from upper-altitude surface scanners should any be turned on this part of Jade. The need for speed was on them, and he wanted no risk of colliding with sudden rises in the land or tall stands of brush with the throttle this far out.

His face was set, his mind sealed, as he concentrated upon guiding the rapidly moving machine.

Islaen was quiet as well and was glad the demands of his driving discouraged conversation. Her thoughts were dark, the look she fixed on the fast-flying countryside was bleak, and her spirit did not lighten as the minutes flew by.

"How you must despise us," she said at last, speaking aloud rather than with mind.

The Arcturian glanced at her. "Why so?"

"First, those developers on Visnu. Now, this . . . thing with the Settlement Board."

Sogan hesitated before replying. He, too, used speech, and it seemed to cost him a struggle to give her his answer.

"I have known the need for wealth since my exile, the desire for some of that which it can procure, enough so to understand a little how the lust for it can infect a weak man's heart. I have not yet been tempted to violate a charge or trust for its sake, nor can I truly comprehend sinking to that even where the mind is warped, but there are those amongst my people, my own caste, who have betrayed humanity and even honor for precious small cause."

"You could commit no treason," she replied quickly. "You're all the best your race has produced, and that is much indeed."

"As you are the best of yours, Islaen Connor, nor are you alone in worth amongst them. I fought many such during the

War and have come to know many more since, and so, no, Colonel, I do not despise you because a few corrupt men exist in your midst."

His mind opened into hers. *There are problems in plenty in this universe, and we seem fated to receive a goodly portion of them for resolution. Let us content ourselves with those and not be creating difficulties where none exist.*

Wise counsel, Admiral, the Colonel agreed and then withdrew into herself again; a vehicle moving at this speed was better for having the full attention of its driver, even one as able as Varn Tarl Sogan.

She was grateful enough for the chance to retreat unobtrusively into her own thoughts for a time. Varn's reply had startled her, or, rather, his manner while giving it had. He had kept his mind tightly sealed, yet even so she had felt an enormous weight of shame on him.

Why, when he had said nothing remarkable? He naturally had felt his lack of credits. He had been extraordinarily fortunate in surviving at all and again in almost immediately acquiring the then derelict-class *Fairest Maid,* but he had certainly known want, probably severe want, in those early months when there was no place to which he could apply for aid, no living creature in all the universe to whom he could turn.

As for having desires beyond the *Maid*'s power to satisfy, that was only to be expected. Outside of the Emperor's own household, with whom he had been closely associated, Admiral Varn Tarl Sogan had been one of the most powerful men in all the Arcturian ultrasystem. Never in all his life before his disgrace, not even during the last months of the War when the Empire was having difficulty in supplying even basic goods to its forces, had he known less than the best, the most superior, of everything his system could produce. Beyond that, he was a highly educated, cultured man with wide interests. It could not but pain him occasionally that he would never again be able to have so much of what he truly loved or satisfy so many of his deeper desires.

The woman gave an inner sigh. The very confession that he did feel such longing was in itself a disgrace to him, and there was nothing at all she could do to relieve his discomfort for having made it. She most assuredly could not be so tactless as to call it before him and try to argue him out of it by putting the name of false guilt on it. Any condition, loss, or lacking which could not be honorably rectified must only be borne by one of the Arcturian warrior caste, held silently within himself. Whatever other mistakes she made in her dealings with the former Admiral, she did know enough not to force the burden of further embarrassment about this down on him.

Maybe some day, it would be different. He had been comfortable enough with her to mention that he had been thinking of his own kin, of his desire to bring her to them, before they had come to Jade . . .

Her lips tightened as Islaen suddenly realized she might be responsible in a good part for the intensity of that longing for greater wealth, aye, and for most of the weight of guilt and shame he was carrying with respect to it. The women of a war prince's harem, and most particularly his consort, were fabulously maintained. It must be a bitter lash to the Arcturian that he could do so little for her, and the fact that she lacked for nothing of real importance and was perfectly happy in her lifeway would do nothing to lessen its sting.

Wounded pride and violated custom aside, Varn was by nature generous. The desire, the need, to give was part of him, and it could only feed his distress that he could not supply her with anything like what he felt to be her due.

A bar of solar steel seemed to rise up within the Federation woman. It was her part to put an end to this, the more so since she had unwittingly caused it, but that would require delicate, subtle work on her part, work which would have to begin later, when this experience was farther from his mind. For now, she would serve him and them better by screening her thoughts, by turning them entirely and fixing them on the task and the potential peril before them all.

The Arcturian kept their speed at near escape velocity, the highest they could maintain on a planet of Jade's atmospheric content and gravity. Only when they at last approached the rough spaceport serving the colony did he finally slow down to a more normal rate of travel. It would not serve their purpose at this stage for them to come tearing in as if some surplanetary demon were snapping at their fins.

At Islaen's request, he brought the flier to a halt on the brow of the low hill nearest to and overlooking the port, now clearly visible in the distance.

He drew back the canopy which their speed of going had required them to keep shut. Kuan Yin was high and her rays, as usual, were warm. Travelers would be moving in open vehicles when the option was theirs.

They turned their distance lenses on the scene below and watched it closely for several minutes. Two freighters were in, and the work of unloading was in full, hectic swing, but there did not seem to be anything untoward in the activity.

It looks all right from here, the Commando observed.

Like a nest at birthing, Bandit remarked, not altogether approvingly.

Better that than too still, Love.—You must be very quiet when we go amongst my people. They're not to know you can talk, and some might possess gifts the Amonites don't.

I doubt that, Sogan interjected. *I believe adoption confers that privilege, which I share by reason of my link with both you and with animalkind. It may be different between gurries and goldbeasts—*

It is, the chick admitted. *We talk to all of them, even gurries who never adopt one do.*

Aye. Your minds have had centuries, eons, in which to grow accustomed to one another. Humans' are different.

Yes.

The man smiled. *In more ways than one, I imagine.*

He grew serious, and he strove to strengthen his link with Bandit's mind. *Remember, though, Small One, our work in this place is grave. It is for renegades that we seek, and among our kind, such creatures can hide themselves very effectively until they are ready to strike. Islaen and I shall have to search very carefully to find any who might be here.*

Gurries do that, too. Sometimes, a predator will go mad, like goldbeasts do, but they don't rage at once. They wait so they can kill even more without need. We sense that, warn the pods, and their own, for they would tear all.

Sogan gave the hen a sharp look, marveling at the growing complexity and clarity of her communication. Either she was maturing very rapidly or she was growing more accustomed to their concepts and thoughtways. Probably, it was a mixture of both, that and her readily apparent desire to please them and share her life with them.

You are marvels, he said, allowing the full extent of his admiration to reach her.

Yes.

There was such self-satisfaction in that and in the purr which accompanied it that he broke into laughter.

The gurry hissed, and Islaen stroked her back. *Don't ruffle yourself, Little Love,* she told her, laughing herself, because the chick's plumes were so extended that they stood at right angles to her body. *You're going to have to put up with that if you want to live with us.*

If I must . . .

The disapproving resignation in her reply set Varn laughing again, and Islaen looked from him to the little hen.

You are indeed a marvel if you can do this for him, she thought. Her lips parted, for Bandit looked directly at her and nodded her head gravely.

Closed thoughts? You can read them, too?

Once again, the Jadite animal nodded.

Sogan did not notice the brief exchange or the fact that the woman had momentarily raised shields against him. He had started the flier once more, and the weight of their mission was down upon him.

It was on the Commando as well. She opened her receptors wide, linking with her husband as she did so. It was not actually very likely that there would be a traitor in the port, but if there were, it was imperative that they know it before making their move, particularly if he held a place of any importance.

TWENTY-ONE

A GREAT RUSH of impressions filled the woman's mind, the inner babble of over a hundred people, each busy with his or her own affairs.

Nothing seemed blatantly amiss, but she had hardly expected to find that and began concentrating on the individual touches of those she passed, seeking blood lust, greed, the cruel triumph she had sensed in the past in the minds of pirates preparing for a major raid, even nervousness or the desire for concealment, the wish to hide from others. She could not read thought, save only with Varn and now with Bandit, but her gift had served her well in the past, and it would serve her here if any enemies were present.

Sogan brought the flier to a stop in the busy central area where most of the populace, permanent and transient, were to be found.

They left it there and began walking seemingly casually in the general direction of the control complex, pausing several times to give greeting or exchange a few words with some acquaintance or other. Both were well known to the Amonites working here and to the off-worlders assigned to help them until the colony was well enough established that they could man the port themselves. Even three crewmen from one of the freighters stopped to watch them pass, for they had been informed by those around them that these two were the leaders and heroes of the already nearly legendary affair on Visnu.

Because both the Amonites and the others were circumspect in their display of goodwill, the pair were rather surprised to hear a loud, hearty call.

"Colonel! Captain Sogan!"

Islaen identified the speaker's mind touch even before she recognized his voice.

Solman Abbott of the Mary Jane, she quickly told her companion.

I remember him.

The Albionan freighter captain came up to them. "Colonel, Captain, it's good to see you. I'd been hoping to find you still here."

"Oh, we will be for a while yet," she said casually. "We're just back from a visit to the main settlement, as a matter of fact. When did you planet?"

"This morning. —Here, let me buy you a drink. It's the least I can do after almost setting a riot on Captain Sogan."

Varn normally would have signaled her to refuse, but his link with the Commando revealed an urgency on Solman that belied his easy attitude.

Abbott either sensed their hesitation or anticipated it. "Please," he added, dropping his voice to a whisper without altering the smile on his broad face. "We must talk."

Sogan nodded and smiled in his turn. "Come on, Colonel. We are off duty, and I did say I bore no hard feeling. It is up to me to prove I meant it."

"We're glad to accept, Captain Abbott."

"Fine!"

The Albionan was about to say more but stopped as his eyes fell on the gurry, who was, as usual, riding Islaen's shoulder.

"What's that?"

"She's a gurry, a young one. Part of Jade's wildlife."

"She's real cute."

"Bandit's that all right," the woman agreed mildly.

Cute like a Terran fox, she thought. She could feel the chick putting forth her power to charm. If the freighter captain had entertained any reservations in his opinion of them, they would be soothed now, and his already apparent inclination to help them would be confirmed or perhaps even strengthened.

There was but one tavern in the spaceport, which, according

to the usual custom, also served as an eating place. The hour was early, between normal mealtimes, and there were only a couple of other patrons inside when they entered.

The three claimed a booth at the rear and gave their order to the waiter, who had followed fast upon their arrival, Islaen asking for a Telvain liqueur, her two companions for a stronger potion popular with the more successful spacers.

She felt her husband's mental wince as he tasted the pale, double-processed brandy. Arcturian officers rarely drank and then only fine wine.

He gave no sign of his distaste, however, and took a long sip before setting the glass down before him on the table. His eyes fixed on the other man.

"You have our thanks, Captain, but I believe you did not bring us here for this alone."

"You believe right."

Abbott fell silent for a moment, searching for words. "Look," he said at last, "we spacers normally tend to our own business and let others tend to theirs."

"I know," the Colonel said dryly, "but I'm a Commando, not the Patrol, and I doubt it's a cargo of untaxed spider silk that's bothering you."

"I don't know if I should be bothered or if I'm being a fool."

"Let's hear about it."

"As I said, freighters don't trouble one another, but there's one kind we all navigate around. They don't carry normal cargo or any special cargo either, at least nothing the rest of us would touch, and they don't carry passengers likely to have the option of riding official transport, but their ships are well serviced, and they're not often short of credits."

"Pirates?"

He nodded. "Anyway, a couple of that type pushed up next to me at the Ribbon Dancer's bar the night before I left Horus—"

"Horus!"

"Aye," he replied, startled by her surprise.

Clever, she said to Varn, who nodded almost imperceptibly, grimly.

Her eyes had a hard, dangerous look now, one they often held when she prepared for battle.

"What happened then?"

"Well, they were pretty drunk, and I guess I was far enough gone myself, but I sobered fast when they came in, if you know what I mean."

He would, the woman thought. Any trouble with that scum was likely to leave one with a blaster burn through the innards. "Go on."

"There's not much. There was a lot of noise, and I might have heard wrong, but I thought one of them mentioned Jade, and the other laughed and said something about space hounds not knocking any more charters out of her. I couldn't figure what would interest them on a little first-ship agrarian operation like this, but I had a charter to bring in, and I remembered you said you were coming here, so I thought I'd try to find you and let you know."

"You acted well, Captain."

He had acted bravely, too. Almost any spacer hearing those tidings would have tried to make a report to the nearest Navy or Patrol base, for no one liked the mass slaughter inherent in a raid, but it was a rare man who would come himself into a region so threatened. The more natural reaction would be to avoid it like a plague center.

"You did inform the Navy?"

"Aye, of course. I don't know whether they took me seriously, but I did get to talk to a Commandant there."

"They took you seriously," the guerrilla assured him. "Help is already en route."

The man's eyes narrowed. "You don't seem particularly surprised. You expected this all along?"

The Commando shook her head. "Not all along. We came to suspect that there was a potential for trouble while we were here. You've given us a time frame."

"You'll be needing help until the Navy arrives. The freighters in Albion's Sector have never gotten any protection from Governor Norgent, and those of us who've dared stay in the starlanes have had practice in plenty in handling pirates."

"Doubtless, and under less urgent circumstances, I'd leap to have another ship to back me, but there are children in the port. I'll want you and that second freighter . . ."

"The *Cotillion*."

"The *Cotillion* to take them and as many others as you can off as soon as possible."

He looked from one to the other of them as a cold chill

spread inside him. Noncombatants were normally just moved away from threatened facilities in the face of possible pirate attack. Evacuation save in the case of some natural surplanetary upheaval was a wartime procedure.

"Just what are you two expecting?"

"We don't know," she answered frankly. "Maybe nothing. Maybe plenty."

The Albionan had more questions, a lot of them, but he quelled the urge to raise them. Now was hardly the time to press his earlier and much activated curiosity about such interest in so early-stage a colony or to ask what had alerted this pair to it.

"What about you? You're not thinking of going up alone in that two-man toy of yours?"

"They won't be expecting a reception committee when they get here."

"Your *Maid*'s hardly more than an oversized projectile!"

"She can give the port a few minutes' advance warning at the least. Even a couple of seconds could mean a great deal. Besides, we'll not be spared in the event of a raid, whether we fight or not."

"We really have no choice," Sogan added quietly. "There can be no thought of abandoning these people."

Solman Abbott fixed him with a measuring look for several long moments.

"Friend, I'm beginning to think you're precisely what I first took you to be, or maybe a bit more. A lot of people in the universe are mad, but only a Commando, a Patrol agent, or an Arcturian officer looks at either death or duty in quite this manner."

Sogan's smile reached his normally cold eyes. "I knew full well that I was marrying the Navy when I married Islaen Connor."

The Albionan's brows lifted. "Well, that was to be expected, I suppose, after what you two went through on Visnu. —I wish you luck. Both of you," he added with a bow toward the Colonel. "The Navy's a heavy cargo, however good the terms of the charter."

"We'll manage," she told him with a little smile. "Federation work has its compensations as well as its difficulties."

"Maybe," Solman replied without conviction. "What do you want me to do now?"

"Finish whatever business you have here and then go back to the *Mary Jane,*" Islaen responded. "I'll be making some kind of move by this afternoon at the latest."

"Aye, Colonel."

"In the meantime, act like nothing's up. I want to give the port a once-over before starting anything."

He straightened a little. "I hadn't thought of that. Colonel, I wouldn't like your job. I don't think I could do it."

"There are times I don't like it much myself, Solman Abbott," she said and then came to her feet. "Thank you. You may have given a lot of people their lives."

"I hope so, though I'd rather be wrong entirely."

He thought a moment. "Would it help any if I were to pop in on the Navy at Horus and tell them to light their burners?"

"It just might. Describe my response to your story. That should be enough to move them if they've been slow getting started."

Islaen Connor went through the port carefully, sifting each reading for its every nuance but discovering no trace of a taint that would indicate infiltration by their enemies. Once she had satisfied herself that there were none, she officially assumed command of the control complex, putting the spaceport on emergency status, and made her transmission to Horus.

To her great relief, she learned a Navy contingent was already more than halfway to Kuan Yin's system, but much could still happen in the forty-odd hours before its estimated arrival, and she pressed ahead with her own preparations. Within an hour's time, everyone the two frighters could carry was gone, and the port was on battle alert.

For perhaps the only occasion in her life, the Commando officer blessed the fact that the pirate scourge was so widespread and severe. Between that and the threat posed by the recent War, no rim-world planet, however poor or recently settled, was lacking in the means of defending at least her link with the stars.

Neither she nor Varn said very much as they drove to the *Fairest Maid* and readied themselves for space.

Only when they began to prepare Bandit for what was to come did they end their silence. Safety webbing meant to support and protect human bodies during lifting and planeting would be of no use to this tiny creature, and Islaen carefully fastened a piece of small-cargo netting to her chair, explaining its purpose to the gurry while she worked. Once it was in place to her satisfaction, she tested it for comfort and showed how to release it should the two humans be incapacitated.

Islaen's large eyes rested on the Jadite mammal. It was into battle that they could well be going, maybe against severe odds, and her heart rebelled against exposing the gentle little being to such peril.

Immediately, the gurry's feathers extended.

Nooo. Bandit will go.

"I won't put you off, but we could be blown to atoms and you with us."

Nowhere safe then.

Sighing, the woman described the pressures sometimes encountered during lift-off. The *Maid* was fitted with Navy-standard drive now, and they should experience little more than a gentle trembling, but it might be different entirely should they suffer damage during battle or be forced to break Jade's gravity chain very suddenly at great speed.

Bandit indicated she understood but was not perturbed.

No danger. Islaen must not worry. Enough other problems.

Good advice, Sogan's thought interrupted. *Strap down. I am ready to activate the engines.*

TWENTY-TWO

LIFT-OFF WAS smooth, nearly without tremor, and the chick freed herself even before her human companions could do so. She perched smugly on the back of the Colonel's chair.

Goldbeasts sometimes step on gurry nests. We stop them, but some weight comes down. Our bodies flatten. Pressure many times our own weight won't hurt us. This was nothing.

Sogan chuckled. *She told us not to worry about her.*

Next, she'll be claiming she can fly the Maid, Islaen remarked in pretended disgust.

Nooo . . .

They attained orbit, and the mood of all three became heavy, Bandit taking hers from her human companions.

Jade's small satellites were clustered together in close conjunction with one another, and Sogan stationed his starship amongst them. To any approaching vessel, she would seem but another of them until the intruder was nigh upon her.

There was nothing more to be done, and they settled themselves down to the waiting, to the constant scanning of the space surrounding Jade of Kuan Yin by eye and instrument, sleeping in turn and taking their meals on the bridge so that human eyes might never be far from the viewers.

Twenty-four hours went by and three more before their vigilance was rewarded. A warning light flickered on the distance viewer indicating some moving object had come within range of the sensitive scanning equipment programmed to function in association with it.

Nothing was visible yet, not even with full magnification, but neither moved from the screen. The newcomer could be a merchantman or perhaps a large meteor or comet or a swarm of smaller space rubble, but the readings showed that it was coming in at high speed on a direct line for Jade.

An hour dragged by before a tiny dot appeared on the very rim of the viewer at nine o'clock, still approaching fast. As the pair watched, its appearance changed from a mere point of light to a larger but indistinct blur.

The woman's lips tightened. Several objects, then. Were they a big meteor with a retinue of satellites, as were frequently to be found in loose association with sun-stars, or was it a small fleet, one fairly large ship and an escort of minor craft?

Another fifteen minutes gave them the answer. A ship, and even Sogan's eyes closed at the size of her. Moments later, the accompanying craft resolved into a dozen, no, not so many, ten, of what appeared to be five-man fighters.

Islaen Connor watched the huge vessel in open horror.

She's as big as a small battle cruiser.

She is a battle cruiser for all practical purposes, her comrade said grimly. *That ship cannot carry less than five hundred, and if she is a raider, she will be so armed as to give every one of them his work.*

The Commando opened her transceiver on both port and Navy frequencies.

"Battle alert. Fleet approaching Jade of Kuan Yin. Flagship of five hundred-class, armament unknown. Escort of ten five-man fighters. Take those out, Port, then concentrate on receiving the flagship if we go down. Evacuate all nonessential personnel immediately. Get them as far as possible from base."

"Aye, Colonel."

The speaker's voice was curt, sharp. He, like the rest of the spaceport staff, had been anticipating a quick raping attack after the normal pattern of pirates, but the size of the enemy craft and the stress the Commando placed upon the need for evacuation revealed at last and all but confirmed the fear which had been gnawing deep within her, which she had not previously revealed.

There could be but one purpose in sending in a vessel of that class to attack an insignificant and poorly guarded colony. This was not to be a matter of looting and incidental slaughter, but a burn-off, the incineration of every living thing, of every seed or spec of protoplasm that might conceivably become or support life.

Jade herself would certainly survive. Only the mighty battleships, the titanic moving cities so huge that they might never leave space and which were the bulwark of both ultrasystems' Navies, only a number of them acting in close concert, had the power to totally annihilate a world's life or even that of a large continent.

That would be of little comfort to the areas the attacker did strike. Nothing, absolutely nothing, would remain where either the spaceport or the settlers' supposed camp now stood.

Her head lifted. Those people down there were frightened, terrified. They had to be, knowing how little they had to throw against such a foe, but their gunners were Navy trained, all of them, and none had been so long out of service that they had lost the spirit the Navy and the War had drilled into them. They knew they faced and would probably meet a burning, awful death, but every man and woman would greet it with hands still upon the firing controls of their weapons, trying even in the dying to take out their murderers with them.

Varn Tarl Sogan watched the ever-nearing raiders through eyes colder than the space outside his bridge. A frigid fury gripped all his being. Those things out there were vermin, all the worst his species ever was or could yet be. At this very moment, they were hastening to carry destruction to several hundred guiltless members of their own kind, not even because of any grudge they themselves bore against them but because one man in his cancerous greed had paid them to do so. There was no thought, not the least qualm, over the lives to be so summarily snuffed out, Amonite or the countless native creatures, fauna and flora, which must perish in any such raid. Few had been so callous even during the War, with all of its many excesses. . . .

A terrible rage filled him as he recalled the touches of some of those nonhuman beings soon to die. Those creatures on the river plain were still called animals, aye, but there was a great deal about them that was patently not animal. Was the attachment Bandit had formed for them not love? Was that goldbeast bull's decision not to hurt Telly, to hear and accept explanation, not the display of a power most like reason? Were these not faculties of mind and spirit, beyond anything normally accorded to beasts?

No matter! Animal or not, they had a right to live unmolested, free from the accursed effects of humanity's greed.

Impotent fury and grief tore him as he realized many, too many, would not survive the coming assault if the *Maid* failed to stop that cruiser. Their numbers were against them. Even if the settlers could make their escape in time, all that vast herd would never be gone from the threatened area before the raiders razed it, not the way they had been traveling, grazing as they went, when he had last seen them. A simple raid would have spared them as long as the colonists did not seem to be with them, but not this.

There was something he could try!

"Bandit, link!"

The gurry started, nearly falling from her perch with the surprise of his sudden summons.

She read the man's urgency and responded to it with quick obedience.

He felt her touch. There was alarm in it but also the desire to help.

"Bandit, can you join me with the herd or the other gurries? We are very far, but the danger to them is great. I must warn them."

Bandit shall try. Gurries protect goldbeasts.

He felt the tiny animal straining, reaching out into a seeming void. Very gently, cautiously, he began giving his strength to her, feeding her effort with his own power.

Still nothing.

Islaen, help us! We are trying to link with the herd.

The Commando joined with him. Her will, her power, flowed into him, replacing what he was draining out of himself, restoring his nearly depleted strength. . . .

At last! Sogan was with the herd and the small flying things that accompanied it.

To his relief, true communication was possible thanks to his attachment to the gurry chick beside him despite the distance between him and the planet's surface, and he quickly warned the grazers to hasten their withdrawal, to leave the river plain far behind before the death weapons of the big starship came within range.

It was to no avail. This peril was too alien to the goldbeasts. They feared no predator on Jade, however large, trusting in their size and razor hooves and numbers to defend them. They did not fear this strange human thing either and were only moving at all because their own human pod and the gurries now attached to it wanted it so desperately.

Despair filled him. He could not sharpen the concept of those far-slaying bolts, not finely enough to convince them, could not maintain the contact much longer at all. The strain of holding it, of transmitting over this vast distance, was nigh unto killing.

The former Admiral put that from him, intensified his concentration. To fail was to permit those below to die.

Images suddenly poured into him from out of Islaen's mind, scenes of the treatment pre-space Terrans had meeted out to the great grazing herds which had once roamed their planet's mighty plains.

The reality of that horror struck deep as the Jadite beasts saw in their minds bull and cow and calf fall, without need or purpose, to lie rotting on the blood-soaked grass.

Sogan had a history of his own to draw upon. Terrans had been savage almost beyond sane comprehension, but all their blood lust was nothing when laid against that which the Arcturian race had displayed in their dealings with every other species which had once shared their native worlds. He knew that grim tale well and gave it graphically, sparing neither himself nor his companions nor the creatures below anything of its horror or what he now recognized as its shame.

His own strength was by then almost gone, but he rallied himself and by utter compulsion of will, he transmitted one more series of images, a nightmare permanently seared into his own memory when he had reviewed tapes of a planetary burn-off just prior to his invasion of Thorne. That poor world's death had left him so sick in soul that he had solemnly vowed never to permit himself or any warrior under him to inflict its like on another. His old life, his honored name, his very seed had perished because of this vow, but Thorne of

Brandine and the other planets in her Sector still lived, and now that infinite wrong his kind had wrought would give life to these ones he was struggling to save. There could be no mistaking or softening the totality of that destruction, or his horror in recalling it—his terror at the thought of even its partial repetition anywhere else.

Neither the herd nor its companions gave him a direct response, but the whole mighty gathering began to move, steadily and purposefully, with no delaying now to pull a last mouthful of the succulent grass.

That image was the last to reach him from Jade's surface. His strength shattered utterly and with it all contact with the imperiled planet.

TWENTY-THREE

THE ARCTURIAN SLUMPED back in his flight chair. His eyes closed, and he moaned despite his halfhearted effort to remain silent. His head was aching as if he had taken the edge of a blaster bolt, and he felt weak as never before in his life. He was tired in every cell of his being, too exhausted to move, nearly too exhausted to live.

A sudden fear filled him. There was no sound around him. What of the others?

Islaen? Bandit?

We're all right, the woman's mind assured him quickly.

Praise the Spirit of Space for that.

Sogan fought to hold the contact. *I thank you both, you especially, Bandit.*

He groaned. *How you creatures of Jade must hate us now!*

Nooo. We love our human pod, and you and Islaen are like gurries to them, but your kind's renegades have longer, crueler hooves than ours do.

Hate, sharp and strong, more piercing than any human's, poured into him.

Even amphibians don't waste like that.

No. That is our work only.

His thoughts ceased. It was more than he could do to maintain even this nearly effortless form of communication.

Bandit gave a shrill, alarmed whistle. *Islaen, help him!*

The Colonel did not answer her. Sogan's first touch had sent her to the *Fairest Maid*'s medical supplies even as she had affirmed her safety and Bandit's.

She was back before the gurry could call for her again, a small, open tube in her hands. She moved quickly to the former Admiral's side and pressed the tube to his lips.

Here, Varn, get this into you.

The stimulant was designed for rapid absorption, and he was sitting up again before he had taken half of it, although he obediently finished it before handing the empty casing back to her.

Thanks.

The woman took it from him rather absently. She had squeezed a minute drop of the yellow cream onto her forefinger before giving it to him and was now holding it out to the chick.

Bandit made no delay in licking it up. She looked from the finger to Islaen and gave an eager whistle for more.

That's enough, Little Love, the woman said with a laugh. *I know you're always ready for a meal, but that's medicine, not food.*

Sogan watched the pair anxiously.

You are both all right?

Aye, his consort told him. *You had by far the worst of it. You originated the contact and were both generator and channel for maintaining it. Bandit only made the linkage and kept it open, and all I did was feed your strength, see to it that you had enough to keep you alive.*

Both her expression and thought darkened. *You could have gone, you know.*

The former Admiral nodded slowly. *Aye.*

He recognized the possible consequences of what he had done, and his thoughts were bleak when he continued.

Perhaps I was a fool, and if I did not violate my primary charge, I came criminally close to doing so, yet I find it hard to lay blame—

Oh do be quiet! We really don't know what we have on Jade, but neither gurries nor goldbeasts are exactly amoebas. Our charge most assuredly does include their defense. Besides, you're full well aware that I can handle the Maid *alone in a pinch. If you had put yourself out of action for a while, I could have taken her.*

Her eyes flickered to the viewer. *I'd prefer not having to do it, however, so if you're feeling better . . .*

Sogan straightened. The intruding vessel had halved the distance between them.

She will be on us soon. The Maid*'s controls are mine. You see to the weapons.*

Aye, Admiral. Her mouth tightened a trifle. *Let's just hope everything works the way it's supposed to work. We won't need any surprises.*

Have you no trust in your Navy, Colonel?

Enough to repeat what I just said!

There was little of light spirit in their banter. It was a conscious bravado, not so much the denial of fear or a display of personal courage but an attempt by each to ease the other's tension, to distract the mind a little from what all too soon had to be faced.

They watched the cruiser cross the face of the distance viewer. There was one instant when she showed upon both the very edge of that screen and the one beside it which revealed Jade's near-space, then she vanished altogether from the first.

The pair had a good look at her at last. She was a needle-nose, slender, fast, with a graceful hull that provided space for a veritable myriad of laser ports.

There was no sign of the last, but there would not be, for no ship would publicize her weak places. Neither doubted their presence nor the presence of a weapon far more deadly, far more evil in its purpose and concept.

She will have strong screens, Sogan muttered.

So will those fighters.

The smaller escort vessels were typical of their kind, light, deadly raiders much favored by pirates and others of their ilk because they could carry heavy armament for their size, and range far enough afield so as not to be too tightly chained to any home base. A wolf pack of ten such ships was a formidable force even without the battlecraft they escorted.

The Arcturian made no move to activate his own defenses. To do so prematurely would be to deny themselves whatever small advantage surprise could give them. The raiders must be brought into range of the spaceport weapons before they realized they faced an alerted foe.

The fleet began its approach.

Sogan ran his tongue over dry lips. This was their first and maybe most perilous test. They must make their initial advance completely unarmored. If he misjudged their enemies, or if he handled his newly outfitted starship less than perfectly, they would be dead before the next three minutes were spent.

Seemingly without haste or suspicion, the tiny vessel drew away from the cover of Jade's moons and turned toward the newcomers.

Sogan opened his transceiver on ship-to-ship frequency.

"This is the Federation Ship *Fairest Maid*. Please identify yourselves."

The cruiser did not bother to reply. A great burst of laser fire tore out from her toward the supposedly unsuspecting government craft.

She was not there to receive it. Even before the former Admiral had finished speaking, his hands had hit the *Maid*'s controls, swinging her away with such speed and at so abrupt an angle that the attacker's crew were left frantically checking their instruments for malfunction.

The tiny ship darted in again, swelling to nearly twice her apparent size as her screens shimmered into place. She dove straight into the midst of the startled fighters, firing rapidly on wide beam.

A ball of light seemingly as brilliant as a miniature star erupted suddenly in the space before them. It expanded, dimmed, and dissipated, all within the space of a few seconds. One of the enemy was gone.

The others remained, and now they grew on the *Maid*'s viewers as their own screens activated. They swept in as a pack to take down their single, too-daring opponent.

They kept a heavy stream of fire on her. The Federation ship's attack might have come as an almost total surprise to them, but the pirate crews were accustomed to battle in space and reacted instinctively to its demands. They had seen enough of her lasers to pinpoint the location of her ports fairly accurately, and any vessel less powerfully defended would already be in grave trouble from the pressure they were putting on her.

Sogan used his starship's marvelous agility to good effect,

and a large percentage of the raiders' beams failed to reach her at all, but he dared not fire again himself. He could readily have blown another of his tormentors to atoms, but to do so, he would have to open his own screens. The *Fairest Maid* would be space dust within seconds after that.

Suddenly, one of the attackers blossomed into a ball of light. Another fireball erupted before the first had reached its full intensity.

A cold smile curled on Sogan's lips. The spaceport gunners had made their move, and they had aimed their blow well.

The rest of the battle would not be so easy, for the port or for the *Maid*. The fighters were scattering, swerving madly to render themselves elusive targets.

The *Fairest Maid*'s chances were different now. Individually, she could take any of them, and Sogan sent her in pursuit of the ship nearest her.

It was not even a contest. Within seconds, the immensely faster government vessel had drawn alongside her target.

The pirate whirled, blasting at point-blank range with every laser he had.

The *Fairest Maid* shuddered under the impact of the multiple strikes, but her screens did not so much as deform, and Sogan felt a surge of triumph sweep through him. Islaen had her targets now, and he knew his ship could take whatever their enemies threw at her until the Commando could capitalize on her knowledge.

Islaen was sitting poised over the weapons controls like some great raptor awaiting the chance to swoop upon her prey.

The raider was in position! Her fingers moved swiftly, and waves of eye-searing blue light burst from the *Maid* to strike the seams where her enemy's screens joined over his laser ports.

The pirate's guards held firmly, but she followed fast with another blast and yet another. Suddenly, his screens wavered. They steadied, but their look was different. They were sprung and no longer formed a solid shield around the doomed vessel. Even before the raider could turn in a hopeless attempt to flee, the woman's hands had touched the controls for a final time, and once again, space brightened with the death of a starship.

More than one fireball contributed to the brightness of the glare around them, Islaen realized. Another was dying somewhere behind them, the remnants of a pirate taken out by the port gunners as he had tried to come after the *Maid* from the rear while she was engrossed in the duel just ended.

The remaining raiders were in flight, frantically seeking to put themselves behind their flagship before they, too, were blown from space and from life. Carelessness and overconfidence had exacted a fiercely heavy price. The fight was gone out of them for the moment, and they were content to let their huge companion take over the struggle from them.

That the cruiser was well prepared to do. She struck at the *Fairest Maid* again, this time hitting her squarely with such a wave of laser fire as should have blown the screens completely away from so small an opponent.

Jade's little champion rocked as would a man struck by a giant's fist, and her force screens buckled and deformed right against her hull, but the Navy designers had done their work well. Her defenses held firm.

Islaen Connor gritted her teeth. Another blast would follow fast upon that first, but she had sighted the cruiser's ports. She would have to time her blow very carefully, but when they attacked again, she would be ready.

All battlecraft were vulnerable at this one moment, when their force screens drew apart to allow their own weapons to discharge. A bolt could sometimes be sent through them to the enemy vessel's grief, or, more commonly, the weak places could be noted and kept under heavy pressure until the seam between the two plates of energy could bear the unremitting stress no longer and tore asunder as had happened to the fighter they had just blown.

It was for the former that she must try. Even the *Maid*'s new lasers could not otherwise batter their way through this monster's defenses.

The Commando's fingers rested lightly on the laser controls, not those she had wielded moments before but on the new purple beams the Navy had installed.

The cruiser spat light, and in nigh unto the same instant, even as that terrible blast swept toward her, the *Fairest Maid* responded.

In the next fraction-second, Sogan jerked her sharply to the left, away from her foe's fierce sending.

The cruiser remained on course. So confident was her captain in the strength of her screens that he made no attempt to evade the small ship's fire.

Islaen had counted upon that. The bolt she sent against her foe was most strange, not a steady beam or lance of light but an eerie stream of minute, violet-colored sparks of almost unendurable intensity. Its speed and the force driving it defied comprehension. As quickly as the invader's firing ports snapped shut, more quickly still did those wee, dire hunters come on, seeking out and penetrating every shadow of an opening.

Most were indeed blocked and ricocheted harmlessly into space, but some few found the trails left by the outgoing beams and followed them back to their ports. The tough solar steel was nothing to them, and within a breath's space after the salvo had begun, the cruiser trembled in a manner terrible to any spacer's eyes, enemy though he be or not.

The guerrilla's chin lifted. Direct hit, and it looked like every port was taken.

Disappointment swept her in the next moment. A smaller ship would be space dust after such a strike, but the invader had survived, although doubtless savagely mauled. She was big enough and her crew was well enough disciplined that she had been able to seal off the damage and fight on.

The woman's eyes flashed. Perhaps, but it would be without her starboard batteries. They were fully and well silenced.

Her attention flickered momentarily from their major adversary, and she scanned the viewers seeking the remaining fighters lest they regain their courage and come in at them at an inopportune moment, but the space around them was clear save for two rapidly dissipating clouds of glowing dust. Jade's gunners were still very much and very effectively in the struggle. Of the final raiders, she could find no sign at all.

The cruiser remained a dark threat despite the loss of her escort and the injury she had sustained, and Varn Tarl Sogan felt the blood begin to race through his veins as the battlecraft's screens brightened and swelled even further.

Here it was, the final challenge.

The former Admiral knew this maneuver full well. He had been anticipating it and dreading it, for although the *Fairest Maid* was theoretically equipped to thwart it, he doubted in his heart that she would be equal to that in practice. She was simply too small, her power too limited to sustain the effort.

There was no choice before him. The cruiser intended to bypass them, to run them down if they tried to intercept her but otherwise to ignore them. The pirate ship knew the spaceport had nothing capable of withstanding her, and she planned to do her murder-work quickly, flaming a broad area around the installation to be sure of finishing off any evacuees, then go on to burn out the camp, land parties to grab the gems from one or more of the most readily accessible deposits while she kept Jade's small defender busy, and then flee back into space, either annihilating the *Fairest Maid* at her leisure or eluding her as the situation warranted.

The Arcturian set his starship directly in the invader's path.

Ready the pletzars, Islaen, his mind commanded.

Aye.

The Commando shifted her position so that her shoulder almost brushed her companion's. The bridge was so arranged that either crew member could, albeit with difficulty, manage both flight control and weapons if need should demand it, and this bank was set closest to that part of the instrument panel normally under the man's charge. Each would have to guard his movements carefully now, for to be jostled at the wrong instant would be their death and that of the spaceport below through their failure.

Fear was a palpable force inside her, a burning bar tightening her chest and knotting her stomach, drawing her nerves taut as wires. She knew what they must do and the risk inherent in that course.

Pletzars were the mightiest weapons in the arsenals of both ultrasystems, the weapons with which the great fleets had battled throughout the terrible years of the War, and only the Navy or Stellar Patrol possessed them, along with a very few private craft commissioned by either service as was the *Fairest Maid*.

No other could be permitted to mount them. Pletzars were awesomely deadly, and screens not specifically designed to withstand their wild brand of energy could hold no more than moments against their attack.

They were, however, weapons of bigger vessels only. Pletzars demanded power. That cruiser out there could supply it, as could many freighters, even those of only three or four-man crew capacity, at least for brief encounters, provided their generators were first amplified to accommodate them.

It was a different matter with a ship the size of the *Fairest Maid*. Sogan had wanted no part of the weapons, and had only very reluctantly agreed to accept this bank as a test. Even with the new drive the *Maid* had been given, he had realized he would not be able to use them for more than a few seconds, very likely too short a time to achieve an end desperate enough to force him to activate them, and the risk he would thereby assume would be considerable. The discharging pletzars would draw every ounce of energy the *Maid* could generate, stripping her of motion, screens, even of light and life-support systems, and too long a drain would make the loss permanent, leaving her a dead hulk entombing her rapidly dying crew.

They had no other course open to them now. It was a chance they must take, and if fortune willed against them, well, the price demanded of them was more than worth the paying if they could only hold in the fight until their enemy's screens went down and she herself with them.

The Colonel had no further time for thought. The cruiser had begun her run.

Islaen's heart pounded. There would be no more massive blasts tearing at them. That space scum knew all too well that even their opponent's weird violet lasers could not penetrate their force screens unless they revealed the location of their ports and gave the *Maid*'s weapon entry by firing their own.

As they must see it, the Federation vessel had but one option apart from withdrawal, that of trying to ram them, destroying them both in a final, desperate effort to save the colony. Of that, they had no fear. Their screens would deflect her as if she were an insignificant pebble, probably tearing out her defenses and detonating her outright in the process.

Sogan let them come very close, until the invader loomed like a small moon in their viewer screens.

Fire!

Islaen's fingers closed on the sensitive rod. As they did, the lights dimmed and then failed on the bridge.

There was no blazing beam this time, just a soft, nearly imperceptible glow diffusing out from the seemingly dead starship, growing stronger, brighter with every microsecond that passed.

Both fixed their eyes on the transparent observation panels. They were scarcely aware of the incredible glory of the onlooking stars in their concentration upon their foe.

For a moment, the cruiser seemed unaware of her peril, then she stopped dead in her charge. Her screens brightened four-fold.

At first, the watchers believed that intensification to be but an illusion resulting from the loss of their own lights, but in the next instant, they realized she had set all her screens before her in a desperate attempt to hold off the pletzar beam long enough for her to reverse and escape out of its range.

Islaen sent her mind forward. It found only fear, despair, and stunned horror, and she quickly withdrew again. She took no pleasure in the terror of others.

It was well that she did so. Scarcely had the Colonel severed the contact than the big ship seemed literally to fall in upon herself as her screens shattered under the monstrous pressure.

After that, there was nothing, nothing save an exploding brilliance that for five long seconds put Kuan Yin herself to shame. When the victorious pair could again raise their eyes to the panels, not even a smear of space dust remained to show that the cruiser had ever been.

TWENTY-FOUR

BOTH VARN AND Islaen sat very still, waiting. Had it taken too long, drained too much of the *Maid*'s own strength?

After a seeming eternity, the lights flickered on, and the instrument panels resumed their normal glow and function.

The woman's eyes closed, and her head lowered.

She raised it again. *Commandos tend to forget what war in space is like.*

Sogan reached out to her with hand and mind. *It is rarely like this. Opponents are usually reasonably matched. I would not for all I revere wish to ever again face a similar contest.*

Nor would I.

Nooo . . .

Both turned in response to Bandit's squeak.

She was still perched upon Islaen's chair but was so huddled in upon herself that she seemed to have shrunk to half her normal size.

Varn swept her up and cradled her in his cupped hands. *The poor little thing was terrified!*

So were we. "I'm sorry, Small Love. No peaceful little creature like you should ever have been subjected to such an ordeal."

Her heart ached. "You'll not have to go through it a second

time. Stay with the herd and the settlers when we go. You belong on Jade—"

Nooo!

Sogan stared at the chick in amazement. There was real anger in that.

"She is right, Little One. Battle is part of our lives, and we have no right to risk you."

Nooo! Renegades can't be left to kill. You must fight them. You need Bandit.

"Thank you, my friend," the woman said softly, and then she mentally repeated her thanks that the gurry consented to remain with them.

Bandit was right in claiming they needed her, Islaen realized. It would grieve her deeply to lose the gurry now. She loved the little Jadite creature, but far more importantly, so did Varn. He feared so much to open his heart after all that had happened to him that she could still scarcely comprehend how he dared to love her, where he had found the courage to permit himself to do so, yet he had also allowed Bandit to work her magic on him. Separation would have been a harsh blow for him.

"Jade to *Fairest Maid! Fairest Maid*, please respond!"

Both humans started, and Islaen reached for the transceiver.

"The *Fairest Maid* here. We have taken no damage thanks to Captain Sogan's management of the battle and to your gunners. If you hadn't kept those fighters off us, we could never have taken out the cruiser. —All of them were blown?"

"Nine for sure. We think we clipped the last, but she vanished while we were busy with her comrades."

"Back into space?"

"We think so, but she might have come down."

"Search for her. She could still do damage, and whatever they be, her crew remain human. We can't leave them to die of want or fall to predators."

"Aye, Colonel."

The woman broke contact and gave her companion a tight smile. *Now for Jake.*

They had no difficulty in reaching the refugees, both the main party and the mock camp.

Karmikel was with the latter group and gave them enthusiastic greeting as soon as they established contact.

"You two are stark mad! What moved you to pit a splinter like the *Fairest Maid* against a battle cruiser, not to mention ten nice-sized fighters?"

"Lack of choice," the Colonel responded dryly. "How did you know what we faced?"

"We monitored your transmissions, of course. They weren't classified."

She smiled. A Commando did not discard training and habit merely because he had elected to leave the service.

"Then you know the whole story."

"Not by a great deal! Hurry down and give us the details!" He paused. "Seriously, come out to us. You could both probably use a good rest and a chance to unwind."

"That we could," she agreed. "We'll be there as soon as we finish up the necessaries in the port. The Navy'll be here by then, and we'll be free to relinquish our guard. In the meantime, you be careful. One of the fighters wasn't a sure kill. She's probably gone back where she came from, but she may just possibly have planeted."

"I know. We'll watch out."

"Good. We'll see you as soon as we can."

Islaen signed off. *I guess that's it.*

Aye. Nothing now but to wait for your Navy.

That shouldn't be long. I beamed our exchange with the port to the relief unit as well, so they know how matters stand.

She sighed. *They'll have questions all the same. I don't suppose we'll be seeing Jake for a while. I, for one, will be glad of the chance to relax when we finally get it.*

Sogan smiled. *We shall have to face a second inquisition first. Your former comrade will not let us off before he has the full story in minute detail.*

That sounds like Jake, all right.

Bandit straightened herself self-importantly. *I'll guide you to the human pod.*

"Jake assumed you would, Love," Islaen told her. "He's just too careful to broadcast our secret openly, just like he wouldn't openly tell us where he is."

She did not find it strange to be speaking thus with the Jadite mammal. Indeed, she almost feared she was phrasing her replies too simply. Bandit had proven herself capable of comprehending a great deal, and she was now a full companion of theirs, to be accorded the same regard and respect as the humans displayed with one another.

The woman glanced at the observation panels and then at both the near-space and distance viewers.

Varn, take us back among the moons. It's a while yet before the Navy's due. No telling what might arrive in the meantime.

He chuckled. *Always a Commando! —Have no fear, Colonel. I had planned to do just that.*

TWENTY-FIVE

JAKE KARMIKEL KNEW by the dim light seeping into his sleeping cubicle and even more definitely by the sharp chill that it was still very early morning, but he could not will himself back to sleep. At last, he sat up with a disgusted oath.

He took no joy in being awake at the moment. He had gone to bed in a foul mood, and morning had done nothing to improve it. He would be hard pressed to keep his ill humor from becoming apparent to his companions today, although in all fairness, the man knew that he must do so. They were not responsible for his discontent.

Jake scowled. These Amonites were farmers, stockmen, but he, through nearly all his adult life, was something very different. He was not accustomed to sitting back and letting others do his fighting for him, and it had nigh unto torn the soul out of him yesterday to crouch here like some sort of defenseless . . . lap pet while Islaen and Sogan had engaged those raiders.

He had cursed himself as a useless coward then, blasted himself for quitting the Commandos when a place was his to claim, but even while he berated himself, he had known he had read himself correctly and made the only reasonable decision open to him. The affair on Visnu had confirmed that.

It was not the continuing risk to his own life which had

moved him to surrender his coveted place in the peace-time Navy but the fact that he could no longer bear the constant, crushing responsibility for the lives of others, sometimes whole communities or even entire planetary populations, which all too often hung upon a Commando's decisions and on the success or failure of his efforts. Islaen Connor had the inner strength to shoulder that burden. He simply did not. Had he remained in the service, he would eventually have wound up putting a blaster to his head or maybe in the clutches of the psychomedics. In either case, he would be doing no good for himself or for the war-torn ultrasystem.

The Noreenan sighed. The involvement of his former commander had done nothing to ease his feelings of guilt and impotence. The thought of her being in such danger, defending him while he had remained planet-bound and in safety, had driven into him like a beam of laser fire.

His eyes closed.

They had been together for so many years, through so much danger and hardship. The friendship and more than friendship binding him to her was not to be severed merely because he was now in civilian life. Not even the fact that she had wed that dark-eyed Arcturian demon could break it.

Islaen was worthy of the devotion she won from those serving with her. She was beautiful, aye, but she was fine beyond any loveliness, brave, clear of thought, compassionate, generous of herself and her resources. . . .

Jake could not say precisely when he had come to love this woman, but it had been very early in their relationship, either in their first weeks together during Basic training or shortly thereafter, and he loved her still. He was enough a son of Noreen and a man of the universe to yield gracefully to circumstances he could not fight, but he still cursed the fate that had allotted her heart and then her hand to the man who had been their bitterest enemy, a man who would have cut her down without so much as a thought had she fallen into his power. . . .

His newborn anger left him.

That was an injustice to Sogan. The Arcturian had slain without qualm, certainly, or, rather, had ordered those under him to slay, but he had never to their knowledge done so callously or needlessly. What was infuriating him right now was not the relationship between them but rather the fact that

Sogan had been in space with Islaen, flying the *Maid* and flying her brilliantly while the guerrilla had handled her weapons. He had ached to be there with them, manning those lasers beside her instead of playing a drone's part for himself by sitting it all out in a comfortable caravan on Jade's surface.

The man threw off his covers and began dressing.

Enough! he thought savagely. He had done what duty demanded of him. He was liaison officer to these people, and his place had been with them. They had been fortunate almost beyond hope that no flaming death had torn down on them from out of space, but it could have been very different. He should have had his fill of danger then, and had it come to that, it was not likely that he would be shivering in this wagon now, whining over his part in the fray.

Karmikel straightened. He should not be doing so at all. He had his own role to play, his own responsibilities, serious responsibilities, and his self-indulgence and self-pity had made him remiss in them. They were not free of peril yet, however unlikely the chance of its striking might be, and it was his to do what he might to lessen its impact if it did come.

Because there was no actual emergency, he waited until the camp began to stir and he saw Telly leave his family caravan to make his morning check on the herd. A gurry chick now rode his shoulder, and he was moving quickly, almost at a run, in his eagerness to greet Midnight after their night's separation.

"Telly!"

The boy stopped, then hastened over to where he was standing. "Aye, Sir?"

"You're on communications duty today?"

He nodded. "I am."

"Good. We're not out of it yet, and I want you to contact the main camp as soon as you think they're up. They're in the outskirts of the highlands now. Tell them to split up into small parties with no more than five people in any one group, find good holes or tangles of brush, and go to ground until they get the all-clear."

"Will do, Sir," he said, "but what danger is there now? Only one fighter got away."

"A ship two or two-and-a-half times the size of the *Fairest Maid* with a brace of lasers mounted in her nose, and space only knows how many more along her sides and stern."

"She went back where she came from!"

He shook his head. "The port people didn't say that. They didn't know it for a fact. She probably has since it would be her soundest move, but if she were too badly damaged to make home port, she'd have no choice but to planet at once or return here."

Telly frowned. "She would need someplace flat and dry to do that, further increasing our chances of meeting with her?"

"Aye, though I'm not too concerned about the possibility of actually running across the wreck. The likelihood of that happening is almost infinitesimally small even if she planeted right on the plain itself. What worries me is that she might spot us from the air as she came in, which might still happen if she's forced to double back."

"What would be the point of killing us then?" the other asked. "If she were so badly battered that she could not make it back home, what could her crew do with the jewels, even if they were able to hunt them up?"

"It's not the river tears. Their only hope of escaping Jade, of surviving at all, would be to destroy the wreck, get to the spaceport as quickly as possible, and convince everyone that they were survivors from a merchantman attacked by the pirates before they struck here. Failure in any part of that would mean either death in the wilderness or execution by the Federation court. Once it was known that the fighter came down, any strangers would be linked with her, and if they did see us, they'd realize we couldn't but have seen them. They'd have to flame us."

"There is nothing we can do, for ourselves, I mean?" Telly asked after a moment's thoughtful silence. "Are we to die as decoys?"

"Your people need these caravans. Since we aren't under a battle threat, or any serious threat save that of possibility, we'll have to get them into the hill country. Once there, we can camouflage them and take off ourselves."

The older man smiled. "We shouldn't be in hiding long. The Navy'll probably finish checking Jade out in a few hours, and then we can call everyone back home again."

"How will we contact the others if the whole camp is split up and in hiding, Sir? We do not have any supply of personal communicators."

Jake pointed to the hen on the boy's shoulder. "The gurries can transmit the all-clear. Between them and their goldbeast friends, they should have the whole company rounded up and reassured in short order."

The chick gave several sharp, aggravated whistles, and Telly began to stroke her.

"I know I should have known that, Baby, but I am really not used to this sort of thing. These human renegades are a great trouble to everyone, worse luck to them."

Suddenly, he looked at the Noreenan in open fear as his hand closed protectively over the gurry.

"If the raiders attack, Fleegee will be killed, too? And Midnight?"

"Very probably," he answered grimly, "and a lot of other gurries and goldbeasts with them. Lasers set on broad beam are not selective about whom they cut down."

"There is nothing we can do to help defend ourselves?"

"Against that kind of armament?"

"You were a Commando!"

"Even a Commando needs appropriate weapons, or at least the makings of them."

Karmikel paused. "Look, I've got something that might be a little help in a pinch, but I warn you, it'd really be no more than a boost to our morale."

"Anything is better than nothing."

"Make that transmission now. It's late enough. After you're done, come to my caravan, and I'll show you what I have in mind."

"Aye, Sir."

The Amonite youth returned to Jake in short order.

"Councilwoman Gaea said they would begin going to ground at once, Sir."

"Excellent. That one wastes no time."

He opened a case which he had already placed upon the table in the wagon's main chamber. It contained the parts of a minute pellet gun.

The Amonite boy looked at it curiously. Even he knew full well that this thing would be of no use against a starship, but he would not insult the other by voicing any protest. There would be more.

There was. In another moment, Karmikel had put a long, very slender metal tube beside it.

He glanced at Telly. "Since I declared myself willing to

work with the military, I was permitted to keep some of my equipment and arms.

"This charge is designed to be fitted to the firing mechanism of a pellet gun and was one of our most potent weapons against small vehicles. What, if anything, it can do against even an already damaged fighter, I wouldn't like to guess."

The Amonite stared at the tube with distaste but also with fascination.

Jake read his look easily enough. "War weapons are nasty things," he agreed, "but it's because millions of men and women were willing both to use them and to face them that you stand as a free man upon your own world instead of kissing dirt whenever some war prince's shadow passed near you."

"Captain Sogan would never have . . ."

Karmikel sighed. The Amonites had reason in plenty to be protective of the former Admiral. He was himself who had at least some cause to be otherwise.

"Granted, Varn Tarl Sogan is the best of his kind, about as close to cultural ideal as any mortal can come, even if his own failed so dismally to realize that fact, but he's still a man of his caste and race. He'd never be a party to excess or cruelty, but had he not been both humbled and broadened by what's happened to him, he'd find nothing strange in making a planetful of farmers virtual salves to his kind, much less see it as a wrong."

"He does not regard us as slaves! He is often cold, aye, but that is only his manner and no lessening of us."

"He knows your worth, and it's to his credit that he doesn't permit any prejudice of his to counteract that knowledge," Jake agreed. "As for the rest, Sogan's reserved, not really cold, and he has reason in plenty to be circumspect with others. You've known fear twice, with the ravagers and now, but he has to live with it. Every time he moves into a crowd, he knows that if he betrays himself or if his race should otherwise be discovered, he could well be beaten to jelly or quite literally torn apart."

"I know. Fleegee explained all that."

"What?" He stared at the gurry. "She knows so much?"

"Bandit told her. She is very proud of both Captain Sogan and Colonel Connor and wants no misunderstanding. . . ."

Telly saw the other's expression. "They meant no wrong—"

"Can they do this with everyone?"

"Only those with a gurry partner or someone gifted like Captain Sogan. —We know not to let anyone else learn about his power, Sir."

"Don't, and don't let him, either of them, realize how much you know."

Jake paused. "Listen, Lad, these partners of yours are all young of their kind. They're innocent and seem to do quite a bit of talking amongst themselves and to you. Every human needs privacy, most of us quite a bit of it, and if you don't teach your little friends very quickly what to say and what to hold close, there will be very few wanting to have anything to do with them. That would be a sad loss indeed for both species."

The Amonite's eyes dropped. Fleegee squawked once, and he reddened.

"They know that already, Sir. Fleegee's tongue was not loose just now. Mine was."

"As long as you recognize that, Telly of Amon, you're well ahead of the game. Let's get this thing put together now. After that, I'd better be quick about readying my caravan, or I'll be delaying the entire camp."

The morning was a slow one, for the caravans had not been designed for rapid movement, and everyone was eager to get to the hill country and the cover it offered, that or else to receive word that Jade was truly free of danger.

Jake did not see anything more of the Amonite boy during that period and guessed he was purposely avoiding him.

He made no effort to seek him out. Telly was embarrassed over the slip he had made and needed a little time to regain his self-confidence. It would be no kindness on his part to deny him that.

In the end, shortly before Kuan Yin rose to her zenith, the herdsman did come to him.

"I wanted to apologize again. I know that what goes on in someone's mind is his own business, and Fleegee and Midnight have both been at me all morning for violating that right."

"They're to blame, then," the Noreenan replied, smiling slightly. "It's time it was forgotten."

"Thanks."

The boy studied him for a moment, his expression grave and strangely mature.

"You Commandos are the equal of your fame, and not just because you can fight well."

"How so?" he asked, surprised.

"You must hate being with us right now, and that comes from me, not Fleegee.

"We felt like dirt, less than muck out of the river, yesterday, cowering here while that battle was going on to save us, and Colonel Connor and Captain Sogan, they are your friends."

Jake gave him a piercing look and then sighed. "Lad, a man does what's required of him. If that weren't the case, our kind probably wouldn't have lasted long enough to learn how to make fire. —Space!"

His eyes had caught a flicker of movement, a dark speck, in the sky above Telly's right shoulder. Even in that bare instant, it had enlarged to the point that its form was all too clearly discernible.

"Scatter!" he shouted to the others. "Spread out and keep running until she turns, then drop flat and stay still. The grass is young and full of sap, and hopefully, the lasers won't start a conflagration."

"What about you?" the boy demanded.

"I'll see if this blasted projectile will do any good. —Damn it, go! She'll be starting her strafing run any second now!"

Telly left him with that, and Karmikel went to his knees so that the grass covered him. Fortunately, he had been traveling a bit ahead of the caravans, and it was not flattened down.

He had little hope of accomplishing much save distracting the pirates from any movements in the grass caused by fugitives who did not freeze quickly enough, but that could be sufficient to buy their lives for some few of the fastest and the luckiest.

The fighter turned at last. Her movements seemed clumsy and were slower than he had anticipated.

She was badly hurt, then.

In another second, he saw evidence in plenty of the damage she had sustained. The steel along both sides was blackened, blistered. She must have drawn all her screens forward over her nose to meet one of the port beams and so far succeeded that it had split, sparing her from total destruction but stressing all her systems, blowing some, and quite obviously sealing every starboard and larboard firing port.

There seemed to be nothing wrong with those in the nose. He saw the cover plates draw back. Soon now, streams of searing light would pour out of those dark holes. The gunners were only waiting to get a little closer, to be sure of their targets. Apparently, the fighter was not maneuvering well, and they wanted to finish the job in one pass.

The former Commando had already slipped his odd-looking weapon from his shoulder. He sighted the starship but held off firing. He, too, would wait a little longer, until she was all but above him. There was some chance of hitting her—either she had no screens left or felt it unnecessary to use them with such prey as this—and he had no intention of wasting it.

If only she held her own fire long enough . . .

Now! His finger pulled back on the trigger, gently, for there must be no jerk to sour his aim.

The projectile shot forth, flying forward and up faster than the man's eyes could follow.

Jake had always been a superb marksman, and his skill did not fail him here. The missile drove home, precisely home, penetrating the very heart of the laser port itself.

In the next instant, the world went mad. Noise and fire filled the sky above him, then jagged shards of white-hot metal tore down, as if seeking vengeance.

The former guerrilla had started to run, but human muscles could not outpace that blistering rain, and he fell as first one and then a second piece struck him hard, piercing him right through the breadth of his body.

The fighter was still aloft, but even as he lifted his eyes to her, she shuddered, jerked once as if in a desperate effort to stay in flight, and plunged groundward, striking very nearly at the place where her destroyer had crouched scant moments before.

Jake was bleeding badly but ignored that as he raised himself a little to better examine her.

His heart sank. It was better than he had dared hope, but perhaps still not enough. She was down, flightless but as yet not fully dead. One laser remained, or its port did, and if any of those inside still lived, as might well be the case since she had crashed from very low altitude, they could wreak dreadful havoc on anything coming within their sights.

Would the Amonites realize that and stay down?

To his horror, Karmikel saw settlers hastening toward him, not all of them, but Telly and some half dozen of the others.

His strength and hold on awareness were both almost gone. He tried to shout a warning, but the words would not come.

His dimming eyes saw the hatch door of the fighter begin to draw back. . . .

TWENTY-SIX

KUAN YIN HAD scarcely lifted herself over the horizon before the Commando flier sped away from the spaceport.

Both its occupants looked tired and strained although they had managed to grab a few hours' sleep. Islaen had been right in guessing that the Navy would have questions in plenty when the relief ships arrived, but she had not anticipated that they would be so insistently pressed.

Because much of the equipment installed in the *Fairest Maid* was of an experimental nature and because of her Commando connection, the small freighter had an extremely high security rating. Her capabilities were not for general knowledge, not even amongst Navy personnel, and the Colonel had claimed Commandos' Right concerning the details of the battle.

That had settled poorly with Lew Ester, the Commandant commanding the relief unit, an officious individual with little use for unconventional forces in the peacetime service and less for specially commissioned civilians. He refused to accept that the guerrillas' privilege of holding the details of their missions close—a very necessary defense for the on-worlders with whom they had worked during the War—still stood, and he so pressed his demands for full knowledge that she had in the end been forced to contact Horus for confirmation of her position.

It had come fast and sharply from Admiral Sithe himself, and with it a direct command that the interrogation cease at once. Ester had been compelled to yield, but he was a small man and had avenged his bruised pride by badgering them both with a seemingly endless stream of needless detail until Bandit had finally exercised her particular magic on him, and he had desisted out of pity for her.

Islaen had felt no small relief when they left the port behind. The experience had been unpleasant for her and many times more unpleasant for Sogan. She had grown accustomed by this time to the resentment some shallow-souled career Regulars displayed against the elite status her unit had won for itself, but the Arcturian had had the threat of exposure shadowing him during the whole of it. He might no longer fear assassination by his own people or incarceration by Federation authorities, but so petty an opponent would have given him a very bad time and might well have leaked the news of Sogan's race to his troops with possible fatal or near-fatal result. The War had generated strong hatred, and there were all too many only too ready to act upon it, particularly if it be with the tacit approval of their own commander.

She looked at the former Admiral sympathetically. His grasp on the controls was tight, and tension was still clearly visible on him.

You can relax now, the woman remarked, keeping her touch light. *They won't come after us.*

No. —That one would have enjoyed clapping me in his brig for a time, and maybe you with me.

Both High Command and the Commando brass know who you are. He'd have been a private doing permanent KP duty before he had set the locks on us.

By whose order? He would have had an ideal excuse for taking full command of Jade, by claiming there was a potential Arcturian plot. He could very effectively ban all interstellar communication.

The Colonel shook her head. *Not a chance. He'd never be able to get to Jake in time. Bandit would've told the herd what was going on. There are other adopted gurries with the colonists by now, and they or goldbeasts working through them would inform the Amonites and him. There'd be a call through to Horus within fifteen minutes, and one on general beam to the entire Navy contingent here in even less time after that, relieving Ester of command. Our people don't like tyrants, petty or otherwise.*

The man smiled. *You're always so certain.*

Of course, at least in this.

Her eyes lifted to Jade's magnificent, cloud-filled sky. *How beautiful it is*, she said softly. *It seems to go on forever.*

In a way, it does.

Sogan sighed. *I wish we were back in space. Jade is fair, but it seems that danger is ever near to us, here or on any other world where we planet.* He sighed again. *I suppose the same can be said of space, and I am but blinding myself to the fact.*

We're just more comfortable there.

The Arcturian gave her a fixed look. *I am more comfortable. You are by training and nature fitted for on-world work.*

She frowned. *Easy, Varn. I chose to roam the starlanes. I love to explore new planets, come to know them and their people a bit, but my place is between them.*

Her eyes sparkled. *Sure, didn't you use that as leverage to get me to marry you?*

Sogan chuckled. *There are times when you refuse to be serious.*

There are too many times when I must be to waste the rest.

The morning passed pleasantly. The day was very fine, almost too warm, and neither felt any need for haste. Jade was a lovely world, made for the enjoying, and they were eager to take advantage of this opportunity to be quiet with her after the tense time just past.

Suddenly, Bandit shattered their peace with a shrill call, extending her feathers to the full as she voiced it.

Renegades have human pod! Jake torn! Killed some first.

"Link me with the herd," Sogan commanded. "Let me see and hear."

This was not space, and the contact was made almost as he spoke.

He hurriedly brought the flier to a stop as his eyes opened to another place.

The perspective was weird, almost unbearably so, incredibly unsettling. Islaen had given him the use of her eyes on several occasions, but she was human and only one individual. Here, his visual and aural receptors both were receiving input from a multitude of alien creatures, goldbeasts and gurries alike.

For several seconds, the former Admiral fought to find order in the vast chaos of impressions, and at last, he succeeded well enough to observe what was happening and know what had gone before.

Only the false camp, the caravans and the relatively few volunteers traveling with them, were involved, praise the Spirit ruling all space, and not the main column of settlers. The toll would not be so high as to be fatal to the colony itself.

Fortune's mood had been bitterly ill, or there would have been no loss at all. It was easy enough to guess the sequence of events which had led to this, and it sickened him that tragedy should strike now, when victory was so very nearly theirs.

Even here, they had come near to winning. Jake Karmikel had brought the fighter down with what had amounted to a suicidal attack, killing two of her crew and taking out one of her remaining lasers, but he himself had been felled, nigh unto if not actually mortally wounded, and the three surviving crewmen had trained their last functioning weapon on the settlers who had come back out of concealment to aid him.

The end was now near. The two raiders who had disembarked to cover their captives with hand blasters were moving back, out of range of the beam that would soon sear the life out of the Amonites, those still concealed as well as the captives.

The muscles of Sogan's jaw were tight with helpless fury, but the princes of his caste were not bred or trained to yield even to the most hopeless situation while life and conscious thought remained theirs.

Jake and the settlers were beyond assistance. The laser would finish them all even if the pirates outside the fighter were overpowered. Any attempt on them would, in fact, only serve to hasten the inevitable. Even Commandos could do nothing to help these doomed people.

That did not necessarily hold true for Jade's native denizens. He might just possibly be able to save them.

He studied the grim scene carefully, silently shaking his head in despair. Several goldbeast pods, those from whose eyes and ears he was drawing the most of his information, were near the scene, too near to draw back quickly enough. The big creatures were patently upset, milling nervously and lowing, knowing something was amiss with the Amonites. A veritable cloud of gurries flew overhead or scurried upon or near the grazers, whistling shrilly and apparently calling to the two presumably adopted chicks he saw with the colonists. The raiders took no notice of them, seeing them as no more than beasts.

A cold hatred filled all his being.

They would not even notice them as they cut them down along with their intended victims. He thought that they seemed to regret the loss of what they took to be the two pets and of the other wild flying things like them, but even the gurries' unique power would have no concrete effect on these vermin, not with their own worthless lives at hazard. The small mammals, sensing what these ones were, might not even have tried to move them. . . .

Determination stiffened him. Something had to be done for them. These creatures with their humanlike sensitivity had to be saved.

Sogan concentrated as he had aboard the *Fairest Maid*.

Move. Move away quickly, or when they slay our folk, you will be burned, too.

As he spoke, his mind pictured the firing of that accursed laser, the death of everything in its path.

The Arcturian gasped. He stiffened, pressing himself tightly against the seat of the flier as if he would force himself through it, his eyes starting, his lips drawn back.

Hate poured into his mind, hate and fury. It was primal in its force, and it was issuing from a billion and a half individuals, gurries and goldbeasts both.

The herd was moving, not away from that which was about to occur but directly toward the knot of humans and toward the downed fighter.

There was no speed in its advance and at first no obvious pattern, but suddenly, the two pirates holding the Amonites went down, thrashing briefly beneath hooves that severed and pulverized bone as easily as they did flesh.

The starship was attacked in the same moment so that she was given no chance to react. Her solar steel plates were proof against hooves, however sharp, but the goldbeasts were huge, and they were powerful in proportion to their size. Queen cows and bulls gathered at her left side, away from the deadly laser in her nose. They pressed against her, worried her, pawed the rich soil supporting her fins.

It took them some three minutes before they toppled the ship. Long before that, all the field in front of her was empty of animal and human life so that nothing remained vulnerable to her save the tall grass. The Amonite prisoners had fled the place, taking Karmikel with them, in compliance with their gurries' instructions even as the assault had commenced.

The fighter had fallen on her side, but the goldbeasts pushed and pounded her until they had rolled her onto her back.

Still, the infuriated creatures did not leave her. Their mighty hooves struck the rich ground beside her, showering clod after clod, thousands multiplied by thousands of them, upon her.

All that anger and fury and violent, dark feeling poured into Varn Tarl Sogan until his very soul writhed under its punishing lash, and still, the flood of it roared on.

There was no escaping it, no shelter left to him.

It was burning the life, the mind, out of him! Nothing could bear this stark rage, the death-wishing of so vast a multitude.

Islaen! She had been linked with him when he had initiated this contact. She was still bound to him, maybe suffering with him! He must save her!

With one last, mighty effort, he broke the contact joining their minds, and then he gave himself over to the horror that was now all the universe for him.

The power to act, to think, returned to the Commando with the severing of the link binding her to her husband's mind.

She herself was all right, for she had not received that awesome flood directly, but Varn could not survive much more of it, maybe no more.

Bandit, stop this! It's killing him, and he can't get free!

In the next instant, the images faded from Sogan's mind, and all awareness with them. He slumped forward against the control board.

The Colonel pulled him back. His eyes were wide, staring blankly, his expression one of pure horror. For a moment, she believed him dead, but then the steady drawing of a breath showed that he still lived.

Lived in body. She could find no trace of a thought, no mental activity whatsoever. By Jade's unknown gods, was this no more than an animated husk that she had before her?

Islaen, I'm sorry! I thought he wanted . . .

"Not now, Bandit!"

She took the man's face between her hands, frantically searching for any spark of inner life.

In and in she went, seeking desperately for any vestige of that once-vital soul, of the one she loved beyond herself or any other in all creation.

Nothing, ever nothing, just emptiness where once a man had been.

There! A barest shimmering did remain, but there was no reaching it, no reaching him. She could not penetrate so deeply, and at every futile attempt, he fled farther from her, so that soon all would be gone, lost forever beyond any touch or saving.

The woman stifled a sob. Varn was still in there. She knew that now, but his peril was great, and she had but seconds left in which to work his survival.

"Bandit, help me. What happened, the terror and massive force of it all, has driven him far back into himself. I can't quite reach him. Help me to do that and to convince him that he can come forth again into a universe that's not hate only."

She felt a gently probing consciousness join with hers.

If only it would be enough! If only he could still recognize these two whom he loved and still had the power to respond to them!

Islaen, your fear is too strong!

The woman gripped herself tightly. If ever a man needed calm, Varn Tarl Sogan did in this moment, that and the assurance they longed to give him.

For a brief space, it seemed that they must fail, but then Islaen's mind grasped his, and the terrible rigidity went from his face and body.

"Bandit," she whispered, "do Jade's other creatures hate humans now?"

Nooo. Only renegades. We love our pod and you who watch over them.

"Are they in a fit state to tell him that? They must be able to come quietly; he's had enough of invasion already."

They can.

Once more, because of her link with Sogan, she felt the touches of Jade's denizens, but this time, they came gently, almost like a murmur, welcoming and sorrowful over the injury they had inadvertently caused.

That soft stream continued to flow into him for several long minutes, then Varn moaned, and his eyes opened.

Islaen?

I'm here.

You are all right? I was afraid I could not break contact in time.

You did. I was fine, too frozen to do anything but otherwise unhurt. You took the full brunt of it again.

His eyes closed. *Poor creatures! What an introduction to humanity they have had.*

No, Varn. They met humans in the settlers. These others were renegades. They know the difference.

What of Jake? He asked after a moment's pause.

He lives, Bandit told them quickly.

He'll be all right, then, the woman said with relief. *Anything the renewers can't repair at once, the regrowth will handle when we get him to the main camp. We'll tell them to ready it when we give the all-clear.*

She smiled at her companion. *He's probably in better shape than you right now, my friend. Here, slide over into the passenger seat and try for some sleep.*

The Arcturian yielded without argument. His mind and body both demanded it, and he knew full well that there was no point in trying to oppose Islaen when this mood was on her. His mind touched hers once, lightly, then he drifted into a friendly, welcome oblivion.

TWENTY-SEVEN

SOGAN CAREFULLY SLID the caravan door shut behind him so that no click should disturb the woman sleeping inside.

He still felt more than a little unsteady even after several hours' rest and was glad enough to sit on the steps giving entrance to the big wagon.

The night was cold and quite windy, as all Jade's nights seemed to be, but the air was fresh and clean, and he breathed deeply of it. Everything was quiet, peaceful, in utter contrast to the violence and horror of the preceding days, and he hoped fervently that this would at last be the lot of the Amonites and of the planet they had chosen for their own.

His eyes wandered to the strange mound standing darkly against the starlit sky. The colonists had worked hard to put the final sods on it just before Kuan Yin's setting, completing the work the goldbeasts' hooves had begun. Islaen's gift had confirmed that nothing living remained within, and she had advised covering the starship over completely and forgetting it. To do otherwise would probably call some unpleasant sessions with Commandant Ester down on all of them and perhaps lead to the betrayal of the relationship between the settlers and Jade's native life.

The settlers would have to take good care to guard against that happening for a while, he thought a little sadly. The fleet from which those pirates had come was a big one, and the Navy would have to remain on Jade of Kuan Yin until they could be certain the raiders had not shared the secret of their hoped-for wealth with any of their comrades. That was most unlikely, but no chance of a repetition of the recently broken raid could be taken. He only hoped, for the Amonites' sake since they wished so powerfully to stand on their own, that the confirmation of their safety would not be too long in coming.

Once more his eyes went to the mound. He thought of the dead men inside, of the doom the last of them to perish had met. His expression grew bleak. At least, they had a tomb and a burial of sorts. There had been nothing left of the other two pirates to bury, not so much as a smear on the churned ground.

The man shuddered but then put the memory from him. It had all worked out well, for Islaen and himself, for Jake Karmikel, for the Amonites, and there was no point in brooding upon the black moments they had endured, although he doubted he would ever be able to clear them entirely from his mind.

He looked up as a figure began to move purposefully toward the caravan. In another moment, he had identified Gaea of Amon's determined walk.

Sogan started to rise in keeping with Federation custom, but she waved him back.

"Please stay where you are, Captain. I am surprised to find you still up."

"I wanted to get a little air and to think for a while. It has been an eventful day."

"Rather too eventful," she agreed with great feeling. "Colonel Connor is inside?"

He nodded. "Aye. I left her asleep."

"She could do with it."

The Amonite woman seated herself beside him. "It is with you that I wished to speak anyway, though I had thought to wait until morning."

He looked at her in surprise. "How may I serve you, Councilwoman?"

"My people owe you and Colonel Connor a great deal. You have saved our colony, and you have given us our lives both here and back on Visnu."

"Councilwoman, do not speak of owing—"

"I do not," she interrupted quickly, "or of payment. There can be no thought of that for such deeds as you two have done, yet a gift may be given freely and received freely between friends. There is not one of us who would see you lift from Jade without some memento as a token of our feeling for you."

The man smiled, softly for him. "You are permitting us to bring Bandit. What more could either of us desire?"

Gaea fondly stroked the gurry cock on her own shoulder. "We could never separate such friends. It would break her heart, and our own babies would abandon us for such cruelty. Besides," she added gravely, "gurries are not objects to be bartered. You taught us that, too. We planned to manage beasts when we came here, and instead, you have opened friendships for us. For this priceless gift, you are citizens of Jade, and Jade is your home and refuge forever."

The Arcturian bowed his head in gratitude.

"I can answer for both Islaen and myself that we are most greatly honored."

The Amonite had anticipated that answer. Multiple citizenship was not the norm in the Federation, but it occurred frequently enough that she had not hesitated to offer them a place on Jade despite the fact that both Islaen and Varn already had planetary affiliations. Indeed, she had known it would be a gesture eagerly welcomed by them. The universe could be very hostile to the likes of them, and they would certainly be glad to know that there was a ready refuge open to them, a world where their history was known and accepted.

She was not so certain as to how he would receive her next gift.

"Please take this. We unanimously voted to bestow it on you."

As she spoke, Gaea opened a small box she had slipped from her belt pouch a few seconds earlier.

Sogan gasped despite himself. A river tear lay within, the largest and most perfect he had ever seen, nigh unto thirty karats in weight and of flawless clarity and intense color.

"There is no way we could accept such a present, Councilwoman. It is a treasure of your own people."

"A treasure whose like nearly cost us our lives and whose existence none of us and none of our children will dare reveal lest some similar peril come upon us again," she replied tartly.

Her eyes caught and held his. "We have studied something of Arcturian custom since our last meeting, Captain Sogan. Tokens of friendship and honor are not only acceptable but are prized amongst the warrior caste, and such usually are in a form adaptable for the adornment of the recipient's consort. Is this not so?"

The former Admiral stiffened.

Bandit! Had that little mind-delving rogue read more deeply than he had imagined and then spread her knowledge to her compatriots in the camp?

He shot a quick look at the Councilwoman's gurry. The cock radiated considerable amusement at his outrage but did not confirm his suspicion.

Blast them all, anyway. . . .

The woman's expression tightened. "Do you consider my folk unworthy of offering such a gift?"

"No!"

His eyes dropped to the gem. "You have guessed correctly—or have been told—that I do wish to have this stone, but how should we explain our possession of it without betraying you? The wealth of an ultrasystem is no longer mine to command, and few lacking very close to that could honorably own such a thing."

She just laughed. "Come, Captain! Each of you earned a class one heroism citation for what you did on Visnu; you shared one for your work over Astarte; and you are certain either to share or be granted individually yet another for that battle you just waged in Jade's near-space. That is a lot of credits, friend, and with the Navy paying for the work on your ship, it is but natural that you would put them into some other investments. Gems are popular with spacers, I believe."

She shrugged. "Perhaps the stone is beyond even that store, but who can say where and to what Fortune will lead, particularly out on the rim where you roam? Greater wealth than this has been found before in Federation history."

The man nodded. Her arguments were logical. Jewels were beautiful, highly portable, and universally valuable, and most spacers with extra credits in sufficient quantity invested in them. Even if Islaen openly displayed this one, no one was likely to question its source very deeply.

He nodded once more and then took the box from Gaea.

"Again, you have our thanks. Please convey our gratitude

to the remainder of your people. You have been generous beyond any right or expectation of ours."

"Just see that you do not become strangers to us, Captain. You are citizens of Jade now, and we expect you to planet here with some frequency, if only so that we can hear first-hand whatever you are at liberty to reveal of your adventures."

She smiled and paused to stroke her chick. "We shall be especially interested in Bandit's part in them."

"It will be a sizable one if her performance thus far is any foreshadowing of the future — We shall do as you request and with the greatest pleasure, Councilwoman."

The Amonite left him after that, and Sogan hastened back into the caravan.

He was about to call Islaen but caught himself in time. No, let it wait until they were aboard the *Maid* and out in space once more. He would show her the stone then, knowing she would understand that Gaea of Amon had made it impossible for him to refuse the settlers' gift. Then he would give it to her.

His head raised.

It was a true gift, a symbol both of the completing of their work on Jade of Kuan Yin and of the beginning of whatever fate and life had next in store for them. Beyond all else, it was a symbol of their unity before all the challenge and all the joy that future would bring them.